THE SUMMER CREW

a tale of salmon fishing on Speyside

THE SUMMER CREW

JOHN BENNETT

First Published 2020
© John Bennett

The Summer Crew is a work of fiction. Names, characters, businesses, places, events and incidents are either the products of the author's imagination or used in a fictitious manner. Any resemblance to actual persons, living or dead, or actual events is purely coincidental.

Spey Publishing Ltd, Kemp House, 160 City Road, London, United Kingdom, EC1V 2NX   www.speybooks.co.uk   john@speybooks.co.uk   fb.me/speybooks

A CIP catalogue record for this title is available from the British Library.
ISBN 978-1-9163594-0-6

1 2 3 4 5 6 7 8 9 10

Designed and set by the author
Printed and bound in the UK by Clays Ltd, Elcograf S.p.A.
Illustrations by Owain Kirby www.owainkirby.co.uk
FSC paper

FOREWORD

I worked an oar on a salmon boat on the River Spey for a season at the end of the 1980s. The events and characters in *The Summer Crew* are fictional, however, I hope it has captured something of that world. There's a short appendix at the back of this book about the salmon and salmon fisheries for those who would like to understand more about the wider context. There's also a glossary to help non-Doric speakers.

The Summer Crew is dedicated to all the salmon fishers past and present, in particular, Geordie, Kenny, Beel, Ewan, Innes, Bob, Stuart, Steve, Ross, Alistair and Angus. Also Jim, who I worked with on the grouse beating. And with thanks to my wife, Charlotte, for all her love and support, as well as my father, Richard, and my mother, Susan, for all their help.

John grew up in Kingston-upon-Spey – the small village that sits to the west of the mouth of the River Spey. He worked on an oar on the salmon nets in the late 1980s, and then did a season as a grouse beater the summer after.

The Summer Crew is his second novel; his first, Sea Otters Gambolling in the Wild, Wild Surf, was published in the UK by Random House, in Germany by BLT, and in the Netherlands by Arena. He's also written for radio and TV.

'That is no country for old men. The young
In one another's arms, birds in the trees
—Those dying generations—at their song,
The salmon-falls, the mackerel-crowded seas,
Fish, flesh, or fowl, commend all summer long
Whatever is begotten, born, and dies.'

WB Yeats, *Sailing to Byzantium*

Reviews of the Summer Crew

"Rarely have I read a book whose characters feel so completely connected to their location, their language and their culture. Not many books have made me laugh as much. A joy from start to finish."

Aschlin Ditta, co-creator
Catherine Tate Show

Praise for Sea Otters Gambolling in the Wild, Wild Surf

"Unforgettable and brilliantly written."

Daily Express

"A fast-moving romp."

The Herald

"Funny, original, stylish, hip, contemporary, funny, daring, entertaining, brilliant..."

Ben Rice, Pobby
and Dingan

CONTENTS

The First Shot

THE OLD RAILWAY VIADUCT rises like the back of some great antediluvian beast out of the willows and alders growing along the broad shingle banks near the estuary of the River Spey. Now carrying only pedestrian traffic on a wooden walkway, the imposing iron arch is a remnant of the GNSR Garmouth to Tochieneal line that ran along the north-east coast of Scotland until, like so many of the country's branch railways, it was decommissioned in the 1960s.

The salmon fishers' bothy that sat in the shadow of the eastern end of the viaduct was, by contrast, an unremarkable structure – little more than a large shed with creosoted wooden walls and a bitumen felt roof from which stuck a metal stove pipe topped by a conical tin cowl. The interior of the bothy was similarly prosaic – in the centre of the packed earth floor stood a pot-bellied stove surrounded by a motley collection of battered armchairs liberated from the nearby dump.

That year, the first day of the summer salmon netting season was warm and sunny, and the air around the viaduct was full of the sweet scent of whins and the faint trilling of unseen larks high above.

Sandy Geddes, skipper of the Summer Crew, leant against the side of the bothy, filled his pipe with a pinch of Alexander's High Society ready-rubbed tobacco and cast his eye over the new recruits standing by the net box. Sandy was a stocky, well-built man with clear blue eyes, a sparse crop of fair hair and a weathered face criss-crossed by a network of thin red veins which betrayed the fact that he had spent the last thirty years working on the salmon fishery at the mouth of the River Spey. Next to him his first mate, Robbie, six foot nine, and almost as broad as he was tall, ran one of his massive hands through his spiky black hair.

'Is it jist me, or div the Summer Crews get werse and werse ivry year?' asked Robbie, turning to Sandy, who was using his thumb to tamp down his pipe tobacco.

'I mean, look at that een there; the een wi the lang hair hauf wey doon his back and thon denim jaiket wi aa the patches and badges on it.'

'I suppose that's the fashion these days,' said Sandy, searching in his pocket for the Zippo lighter his niece had given him for his fiftieth birthday.

'Aye, but fit kind o fashion is it that maaks ye look like a quiney?'

'Sorry Robbie, yer asking the wrang boy; I wouldna hae a clue.'

'I mean, faur dee they get them fae?' asked Robbie.

'Weel, the een wi the lang hair, he's Dorothy's loon.'

'Nivir,' exclaimed Robbie with some astonishment, 'Dorothy Lumsden? Fae Nether Dallachy?'

'The same,' said Sandy, lighting his pipe.

'Fit mist she think, wi him roamin aroon looking like at?' said Robbie shaking his head.

'I would have thocht she wis quite proud o him; he's at the University in Aiberdeen.'

'And thon ither boy, wi the spiky hair and the ripped sark, fa's he?'

'Dee ye mind Beel Thom? Worked for the Hydro Board. Went doon te England aboot ten year ago.'

'No, but I kaent his faither, aull Beel.'

'Aye, weel, that's young Beel's loon, he's up for the summer. He's at the University in Aiberdeen as weel.'

'Dee they aa gan te the university these days?' asked Robbie as Sandy exhaled a large puff of smoke.

'I nivir understood fit the point o that wis,' continued Robbie, 'we baith left the school at the age of fourteen and it nivir deen us ony herm.'

'Aye weel, it's changing times, Robbie, changing times.'

'Should there nae be anither een?' asked Robbie, looking perplexed, 'I mean, there's us twa fae the permanent crew, the regulars, Jake and Corbie, thon twa gowks by the net box...but that still means we're a man doon.'

Sandy took another long, considered puff of his pipe, but before he could answer Robbie's question, a tractor appeared on the track which led from the road to the bothy. The tractor, an old Fordson Super Major, leprous with rust, was towing a trailer carrying a coble – the large, flat-bottomed rowing boats used in the salmon fishery; at the wheel of the tractor was Brian, temporary skipper of the permanent crew.

'Well, there's the answer to yer question,' said Sandy, pointing at the tractor with the stem of his pipe.

'Fit? Brian?' said Robbie, looking confused, 'he's skipping the permanent crew...'

'No, nae Brian, look at the back o the bogey.' As the tractor swung up onto the grass by the bothy Robbie spotted the passenger – a fair-haired, moon-faced boy of about eighteen – sitting on the back of the trailer with his hand in a bag of pickled onion Monster Munch.

'Och no, it's nae is it?' said Robbie, unwilling to believe his own eyes. Sandy nodded his head.

'Nae the Neap...'

'Aye weel, it's fa ye kaen, nae fit ye kaen that coonts in this life,' said Sandy philosophically.

Neil 'The Neap' MacKenzie was the only child of the Superintendent, Sampy McKenzie, one of the men in charge of the salmon fishery; consequently, the Neap was well known to the permanent employees. In fact, he had briefly worked on the salmon fishing earlier that year, before coming down with a particularly nasty case of gastroenteritis, after a visit to the Bombay Duck Indian restaurant in Buckie. However, during his short spell on the crew he had made quite an impression, and it was generally agreed that he was almost certainly the laziest and most useless person to work on the salmon fishing in the many hundred years of its recorded history. As Robbie said, exaggerating only slightly, 'the only time his hands left his pooches wis fan he wis pitting food in his moo.'

After the Neap had struggled off the trailer – he was large and in not very good shape – Brian backed it down the broad shingle bank – which the locals call the scap – and into the water where Robbie and he floated the coble off. After tying up the boat, Sandy, Robbie and Brian convened around the door of the bothy.

'So Sandy, is it a bet yer efter?' said Brian clapping his hands together and looking over at the Neap who had, to the astonishment of the two students, just managed to put three whole, intact Wagon Wheels in his mouth simultaneously.

'Aye weel, I suppose so,' said Sandy, without much enthusiasm.

'Och, ye might as weel gies the money the noo,' said Brian, rubbing his hands together.

'Mind, ye lost last year…' said Sandy, remembering the case of whisky the Summer Crew had won from the permanent crew the year before, having caught six boxes of fish more than them over the course of the summer.

'Aye, ye've got an awfa short memory,' said Robbie.

'Aye, and ye've got the Neap,' replied Brian.

Robbie and Brian did not get on, partly because Robbie was still smarting that he had not been made skipper of the permanent crew when Sandy temporarily vacated the job to take charge of the inexperienced Summer Crew. After all, Brian had been on the fishing for only three years, and, unlike Robbie, had little idea of where the fish lay or when it was best to shoot the river. However, Brian was married to the Super's sister, and, as Sandy had already noted, the salmon fishing was not a strict meritocracy. To be fair to Robbie, envy wasn't the only reason for his dislike; most of the other salmon fishers found Brian quite hard going too, for he was one of those men who had been everywhere and done everything and, if you were in his company you only had to mention the fact that you'd had a tin of pineapple rings for your supper and he would be off on some anecdote about 'the time fan we wis unloading a cargo of steel in Honolulu…' because Brian had, before joining the salmon nets, spent twenty years in the Merchant Navy. Tales of far off lands, told occasionally, with a dash of self-deprecation, can enliven a long shift, however, it can be wearing being stuck in a bothy on a cold, sleety night in April listening to the tale of the Bangkok ladyboy for the fifteenth time.

'There's nae wey we're losing te him,' said Robbie, anger flashing in his eyes as the tractor disappeared through the trees behind the bothy.

'Aye weel then, in that case ye'd best get thon twa new boys sorted oot,' said Sandy, 'oh and by the by, the Neap's on an oar wi you.'

'Fit?' said Robbie incredulously, 'I thocht that we'd pit the Neap on the sting…'

'That's fit I wid hiv deen, but the Super wants him teuchened up.'

Robbie shook his head, 'it's g'te be a lang summer,' he said, half to himself.

*

Robbie ran the new recruits through the rudiments of netting the river as Jake and Corbie loaded the net onto the back of the coble. When the net was on board, Sandy instructed all of the Summer Crew to get into the coble, so they could go down to the slower Lower Bridge Pool where it would be easier to show them the ropes.

'Sandy,' said Robbie checking the stroke of his oar as the

boat reached midstream, 'is there nae oer muckle watter in the bilge?'

'Jake, gie her a wee go wi the bailer,' said Sandy looking down from his position by the net at the back of the boat. Jake, a short man with fair hair and a wiry build who ran a small croft in Clochan and supplemented his income working on the salmon fishing during the summer, grabbed the bailer and started work. However, thirty seconds later the rate of ingress had increased dramatically and despite Jake's best efforts, the water was suddenly up to the ankles of the Summer Crew's waders.

'Robbie, taak her in, taak her in,' said Sandy urgently, slipping his pipe into his pocket.

Robbie, straining every muscle in his huge back pulled at his oar, unfortunately the Neap, who was on the other oar, caught a crab and fell backward into the rapidly filling bilge causing the boat to spin round so the stern was facing downriver toward the onrushing rapids at the bottom of the pool. Robbie grabbed the Neap's oar and pulled hard toward the bank as the Neap floundered around in the bilge.

'Hey, you wi the short hair, get oot and land the boat,' shouted Sandy, as they drifted over a small spit of shingle running out from the far bank.

The short-haired student grabbed the rope attached to the prow of the boat and jumped overboard into the river. And while the water wasn't particularly deep, it and the coble were moving quickly, so he barely managed to stay on his feet as the coble swept on down towards the brae at the bottom of the pool pulling him behind it like a water skier. As he held onto the rope the water splashed up dangerously close to the tops of his waders, and for a moment he almost let go to save himself from being pulled under, but just as he was about to release the rope, the water suddenly became shallower so he held on, leaned back and dug his heels into the shingle.

The Stingman's actions didn't stop the boat entirely, but they slowed it enough to let Jake and Robbie jump out and grab the wooden rollocks. The Stingman relaxed slightly as they took the strain, which was a mistake, as he tripped on a rock then fell forwards face-first into the river.

As the Neap rung his t-shirt out, Robbie came up to the Stingman who was emptying his waders out onto the scap.

'Aye, yer looking a wee bitty drookit there,' he said, clapping the short-haired student on the back and severely winding him in the process.

*

The official enquiry was held that evening in the Super's office, down by the icehouses at Tugnet. As they were waiting for the Super to call them in, Brian taunted Sandy.

'So you went down wi the boat did ye? I heard ye aa wint fur a dook,' said Brian, laughing loudly.

'Verra funny,' said Robbie, 'ye kaent fit wis gan on, did ye?'

'I kaent nothing aboot it. It was aa the Neap's fault.'

'That's a wheen o havers min,' said Robbie towering over Brian.

'If ye hit me then I'll get the bobbies on te ye; I've got witnesses,' said Brian nervously. Fortunately for Brian, the Super appeared in the door and called them through.

'OK, so fit happened?' he asked, leaning back in his chair and lighting a cigarette.

It didn't take long for Sandy to explain why the boat had gone down, for the cause was quite clear. A coble needs to stand in the water for a week or so to let the dry clinker planks swell up and form a watertight seal, which is why all the cobles on the Spey salmon fishery were purposely sunk and then held down with heavy rocks for about a week before use. The coble that Brian had delivered to the Summer Crew was a dry coble, and though it had floated well when it was empty, as soon as the crew embarked, the extra weight, and therefore pressure, opened up the dry clinkers and let the water flood in.

'Brian delivered the wrang coble,' concluded Sandy.

'No, no, no, that's nae true,' protested Brian.

'Are you saying it was deliberate?' asked the Super, ignoring Brian, 'because if ye are, Sandy, that's a very serious accusation; we lost a hale day's catch there.'

'All I'm saying is that it wis definitely a dry boat. And there wis nae wey we could tell until we actually got in. I mean, it could hae been a hale lot werse: we could easy o cowped the boat…then fa kaens fit wid o happened.'

'But it wisna my fault,' said Brian, 'it wis the Nea…it wis young Neil fa telt me fit coble te taak.'

'Is that right?' asked the Super after the Neap had been summoned from next door where he'd been watching *Smokey and the Bandit* on the video.

'I suppose so Dad, but I forgot fit een you telt me te taak and I didna kaen it wid maak ony difference,' said the Neap lending much credence to Sandy's earlier assertion that in this life it's who you know, not what you know, that counts.

Stots and Bangs

SANDY GEDDES, skipper of the Summer Crew, stood by the netbox, watching the young recruits loading the net onto the back of the boat. With him were the three senior members of the crew – Robbie, Jake and Corbie.

'Och I canna watch,' said Corbie shaking his head, 'they're maaking a richt fankle o thon net.'

Colin 'Corbie' Cameron was a tall, thin awkward looking man with a pronounced pecking gait when he walked, which along with his black hair, earned him his nickname. Corbie shared a small cottage with his older brother in Garmouth and had worked on the Summer Crew for over ten years, but, possibly because of his rather irascible nature, he'd never been offered a permanent job, a fact that only served to exacerbate his ire.

'Aye, the last shot wisna guid,' said Sandy pensively.

'It started fan the Neap cocht a crab jist as we turned

doon stream,' said Robbie.

'We've cocht mair crabs than we hiv fush fan he's on the oar,' observed Corbie bitterly.

'Aye weel, there's nithin we can dee aboot young Neil,' replied Sandy quickly, still looking down at the younger members of the crew struggling with the net.

'And that een wi the lang hair wis bleezin again last nicht, that's twa o the first three nichts,' said Robbie.

'Students,' said Corbie contemptuously, 'they're nae yees fur nithin, they're jist bone idle.'

*

It was true that the new recruits to the Summer Crew were struggling to learn the ropes. Salmon netting is, in essence, a relatively simple affair: you have a net, you put it on the back of a boat, three of the crew stay on the bank and hold the free end of the net while the four others row round the pool paying out net all the way. When those on the boat have rowed the length of the pool and back to the bank they started on, they jump out and the two groups, holding either end of the net, then haul it in, killing any fish they catch. However, like many things that are simple in theory, salmon netting is much harder in practice – there's a lot to learn about handling a boat, working with ropes and nets and staying safe in the river, all of which is made harder on the Spey because it's the fastest flowing river in Scotland. And it's not just the speed of the water that makes the Spey hard to fish – below Fochabers the river spreads out into a wild landscape of rapids, pools and shingle braids dotted with small stands of broom, whin and willow. Fishing this part of the river can be tricky as the boats frequently have to be hauled over the shallow shingle braes and can easily snag their gear on the broken trunks and limbs of trees washed into the river by the frequent spates. And then finally, as if all of that weren't enough, the new recruits also have the physical challenge of keeping up with the permanent members of the crew, which is hard because salmon netting seems to require the use of muscles that even the fittest men never knew they had.

*

'Och, come oan boys,' said Jake who had until this point kept his counsel, 'granted they're nae that guid yet, but they've nae hid mich time, and young loons is aye ge te ge oot on a spree fan they get the chance. You canna hae a pop at them fur at. Mind fan we wis young, Robbie? We wis like McGinty's pig.'

Robbie frowned, 'weel, I kaen fur a fact that Brian and the permanent crew is oer fowr boxes aheid of us aridy.'

'Robbie, it's the same iviry year, the first wik the young loons is aye oot o their depth. Yer being oer hasty like the young loons, ye need te ca canny and ignore Brian. Ye've nae idea fit these boys is capable o yet.'

'I kaen fit yer saying, Jake,' said Sandy before taking a thoughtful puff of his pipe, 'but I'm nae so sure aboot this lot...'

'The Stingman wis OK on the first shot, fan the coble went doon...' said Jake. Sandy nodded and scratched his chin.

'Aye, but he fell in, and he's nae been guid since, I vote we replace him and the ither een,' said Robbie, 'if we canna get rid of the Neap, we're ge te need aa the guid werkers we can get to maak up fur him.'

'Aye, but fa wid we get?' asked Sandy.

'Weel, I happen te kaen that the Stot is aroon the noo,' said Robbie, 'I seen him ootside the Redder in Fochabers yisterday, apparently he's back fae the boats. He's a guid werker fae fit I heard, dee twice as mich on his ain as thon twa numpties pit thegether.'

Peter Grant, commonly known as 'the Stot', hailed from Buckie. A tall, thick-set man who, while not quite as big as Robbie, was well over six foot and instantly recognisable on account of his shock of red curly hair and the large silver nose ring that pierced his septum and gave him his nickname. The Stot usually worked on the offshore fishing boats, though he had worked on the salmon fishing for a short spell a couple of years before.

'Och nae him, he's a total heider,' said Jake, 'you nivir hid te werk wi him, I did...'

'Aye, fit happened te him the last time...did he nae get his jotters?' asked Sandy.

'Nae exactly,' said Jake, 'he went on the randan efter getting peyed ae wik...mind it wis fan he hid that stramash on the Plainstanes at Elgin, it took fowr bobbies wi batons and teargas te taak him doon. The Sheriff gied him six wiks in Porterfield, and by then the Summer Crew wis oer an deen wi...'

'But he wis a guid werker fae fit I heard; a richt herdy scone...' said Robbie.

'Oh aye, he'd dee the werk of twa men, but he's totally feil,' said Jake, 'abdy wis feart o him...an I kaen fur a fact that the only reason he's aroon is that he's been thrown aff anither affshore boat and there's nane of them desparate enough to taak him on the noo. It'd be gey risky taaking him back.'

'Fit about Jimmack fa werked the nets at Portsoy?' said Sandy.

'I'll gee him a ca,' replied Robbie, 'and ma cousin Cecil wid probably dee it, he's fencing in the wid the noo, but I think he'd jack it fur the fushing.'

'OK, so is that a decision?' asked Corbie.

Sandy looked pensively over towards the new recruits who were still struggling with the net.

'I'll say it again, I think we're being oer hasty,' interjected Jake, 'ye've nae hid time te judge them...'

'Aye weel,' said Sandy, 'let's see if the ither boys is free afore we dee onything. We can maak a decision on Seturday.'

As Sandy spoke, a shiny new Toyota Hilux pickup truck pulled into the clearing by the bothy. A short, brown-haired man with voluminous sideburns got out of the truck, cast a quick look around, and then started loosening the rope that held the tarpaulin over the flatbed.

'Who's that?' asked the short-haired student, who had drifted over to see what was going on.

'That's nane o yer business, is fit it is,' said Corbie sharply, before he, Sandy, and Robbie walked over to the pickup and shook hands with the driver.

'That,' said the Neap, joining the short-haired student by the bothy, 'is the boy fa sells the broonic.'

*

In his influential 1902 book, *The Salmon Rivers of Scotland*, Augustus Grimble wrote,

'There is no question…that the last nine miles of the River Spey, from Boat o' Brig to the sea, is the finest and most productive stretch of water in Scotland.'

And the fishing on the Spey is not just well regarded in Scotland, it is undoubtedly one of the most famous salmon rivers in the world. However, despite its fame amongst the fishing fraternity, it is probably fair to say that it is for its whisky that the Spey is best known. Many whisky aficionados are of the opinion that the distilleries of Speyside make the best whisky in the world, and while there are those in Ireland, America, Japan and even Scotland itself who would no doubt debate that assertion, what is incontestable is that the Spey and its tributaries are home to over fifty of the world's most famous single malts including Macallan, Glenfiddich, Glenlivet, Cragganmore, Dalwhinnie, Balvenie, Glenfarclas, Aberlour, Cardhu and Tamdhu, as well as the best parts of blends like Johnny Walker and J&B Rare: a concentration like no other in the world. In other words, Speyside is to whisky what the Burgundy region of France is to red wine.

Whisky distilleries have now become mechanised wonders operated by computers and a handful of men. However, before the computer age many distilleries still employed a large workforce, many of whom got thirsty from time to time. And while these men were often scrupulously honest in other aspects of their lives, they were, on occasion, known to help themselves to the odd dram or two of whisky without necessarily asking the management for permission. Before you pass judgement on these men, you should know that their actions weren't purely selfish – many of them, no doubt motivated by feelings of sympathy for their fellow man, were willing to share, in return for a small consideration, the whisky that occasionally found its way into their possession. Of course, the distilleries and the excisemen did their best to discourage such altruism, however, it turns out that whisky is one of those substances that it is very hard to contain in one place so, despite the best efforts of the authorities, it was always getting out of the distilleries by one means or another.

There are two main types of illicit whisky that find their way out of distilleries – broonic and clearic. Broonic is taken from the casks ageing in the bonded warehouses; it is usually about 70% proof and is, as the name suggests, brown. Clearic is the raw grain spirit taken before it is casked; it can be up to 90% proof, and is, as the name suggests, clear.

'Are you not getting some whisky?' asked the short-haired student turning to Jake.

'No, I dinna drink ony mair – it disna agree wi me,' said Jake shaking his head, 'though I suppose ye cud say, mair accurately, it maaks me disagree wi ither fowk.'

The new recruits watched as Sandy, Robbie and Corbie filled four empty whisky bottles each with broonic from the spigot in one of the large plastic containers in the bed of the pickup.

'De ye think he'll let us buy a bottle?' asked the long-haired student.

'Ye can aye ask, but I widna get ma hopes up oer much, he'll nae sell it to onybody he disna kaen,' replied Jake.

The long-haired student walked over and tried his luck, only to be sharply rebuffed by Robbie.

'Ye've been fou twa o the last three nichts, there's nae wey yer getting ony broonic or clearic. Besides, you young loons widna be able to hannel it.'

And there was some truth in this. It is very easy to underestimate the strength of broonic or clearic and drink far too much, too quickly as many have found to their cost. However, the younger members of the crew weren't so easily put off.

'That's nae fair, we've got the spondulicks,' complained the Neap.

'You boys need te focus on yer fushing, afore ye're awa getting fou. This wik is a trial, mind,' said Sandy sternly, 'and ye need te prove yer werth. There's nae guarantees we'll keep ye on.'

*

The rain which had started as a smirr just after lunch developed into a heavier and more persistent downpour by the end of the shift. The final haul of the day was a nugatory affair, and there was a quiet, pensive air about the crew as they hauled the boat back up to the bothy through the rain. The new recruits now worried about Sandy's earlier warning; the older members of the crew concerned they had all but lost their bet with Brian already; and Sandy undecided what to do about the new recruits.

As they approached the bothy, it was Sandy, at the head of the tow-rope, who first spotted the unmistakable figure of the Stot leaning against the netbox. As the crew approached the bothy, it rapidly became apparent that the Stot was considerably the worse for wear.

'Fit like, Robbie?' he said, slurring his words and holding onto the netbox as if it were the gunwale of a deepsea trawler pitching in a force eight gale 50 miles off Peterhead.

'Aye, nae bad,' said Robbie cautiously as he tied the boat up.

'So fan dee I start, Sandy? I'm raring te go, I could dee a shot noo,' said the Stot still riding the swell.

'Aye, weel, I'm nae sure…' said Sandy hesitantly.

'Hae ye geen the ither boys their jotters?' continued the Stot, looking around the rest of the crew.

Sandy looked over at Robbie. Robbie looked shocked, clearly as surprised as Sandy by the Stot's announcement.

'Fit are ye nae so sure aboot?' said the Stot steadying himself.

'Weel, there wis a possibility…it wis never, eh, ye kaen,' said Sandy circumnavigating the point.

'Are ye sayin there's nae job? That's nae fit Robbie telt me,' said the Stot, his bonhomie suddenly switching to belligerence in the way that it can in the very drunk. 'He telt me that it wis a shoo in, I've come aa the wey doon here in guid faith, and aa yer deen is thrawn it back in ma face.'

Sandy tried to placate the Stot, 'look Peter, we dinna wint ony trouble.'

'I wis telt there wis a job…' said the Stot lurching towards Sandy aggressively. As he did Robbie stepped forward and put his hand on the Stot's shoulder to stop him.

'Look, we're nae needin ony…' but before Robbie could finish his sentence, the Stot had swung round on his toes and delivered a surprisingly accurate right hook that landed on Robbie's temple and knocked him onto his backside. As he sat there, dazed, the Stot baited him, 'Aye, Robbie, and fit are ye ge te dee aboot it? Come oan, I've ayeweys kaent I cud taak ye, let's hae a square go. I dinna care hoo mich bigger ye are.'

The rest of the crew froze, unsure what to do next, apart, that is, from the long-haired student, who stepped forward.

'Peter, wid it nae be better te get oot o this dreich weather, and taak a seat in the bothy and hae a dram or twa and werk it oot?' he asked.

Sandy and Jake looked at each other nervously. The long-haired student was seemingly unfazed by the menacing figure of the Stot. Robbie pulled himself slowly to his feet.

'Sandy, if ye dinna mind, I'll get Peter a dram, if ye get a couple o sticks fur the stove,' said the student looking pointedly at Sandy, 'noo, come on Peter, let's git ye a dram.'

To the great surprise of the rest of the crew the Stot put down his fists and followed the long-haired student into the bothy, where he flopped back into one of the armchairs. The long-haired student poured a generous dram from the emergency bottle of broonic that Sandy kept under the old nets at the back of the bothy, and put the bottle down on the hearth of the stove.

'Richt, I'm just awa te get the sticks fae Sandy, it's a wee bitty caal in here,' he said, backing swiftly out of the bothy as the Stot downed his whisky in one gulp. As soon as he was out of the bothy the long-haired student closed the door, quietly dropped the lock bar in place, and then slipped the padlock through the hasp.

'Sandy, pass me the keys, just to make sure,' he whispered.

'Hey, fa pit oot the licht?' mumbled the Stot. Sandy fished the keys out of his pocket and handed them to the long-haired student.

It took a couple of minutes for the Stot to realise what had happened. His reaction was predictable.

'So, noo ye've cocht a foggie bummer in yer haun, fit are ye ge te de? It it'll nae be oer lang afore it stings ye,' said Jake smiling at the long-haired student, as the Stot hurled himself against the door of the bothy again.

'I'll smash this fucking place te kinlin,' howled the Stot, shifting his point of attack and starting to kick at the walls. 'And then I'll hae the lot of ye.'

The bothy was a sturdy structure built to keep out the people who periodically tried to break in, however, it was not designed for incarceration and it was clear that it was only a matter of time before the Stot broke free from his temporary prison.

'So come oan then, student, fit's the plan?' said Jake as he leant against the door in an effort to hold the Stot at bay.

'Sandy, get the two-way radio from your car, speak to the Super and get him to call the police,' said the long-haired student.

'If ye clipe on me te the bobbies, ye'll nivir hear the last of me. I'll hunt ye aa doon and thrash ye,' roared the Stot who'd clearly been listening to the chat outside the bothy. Sandy looked uncertainly at Robbie who was still rubbing his temple, looking dazed. It was then that the short-haired student stepped forward.

*

The Summer Crew stood and watched as the Stot swayed along the rough track that lead from the bothy to the road.

'Aye, he's using the fill width o the road,' observed Jake, 'I'd say he wis odds on te drap at least ane o thon plastic bugs he's cerrying.'

'I hope he draps baith o them and faas on the gless,' said

Corbie uncharitably, 'I canna believe the students his geen awa oor broonic.'

For that was the solution hit up on by the short-haired student. When the idea was first floated it met considerable resistance, however, Sandy had no desire to either call the police or let the Stot out and get into a fight with the Summer Crew which would probably have ended up with the police being called anyway. Any involvement of the law would inevitably have reflected badly on the Summer Crew and therefore on Sandy himself, something he was keen to avoid after the debacle of the first shot earlier in the week. It was also clear that Robbie bore some responsibility for the Stot's assumption that there was a job opening, so he didn't complain too much. Corbie, who had been much more voluble in his opposition to the plan, fell into line after Sandy offered to recompense him the next time the broonic man came around. Though he still wasn't happy.

'Fit if he comes back again? We've jist shown him we're feart o him, and noo he'll be back the morn or next wik speiring us fur mair drink; he'll be like the mafia, back again and again.'

'I widna think so,' said Jake, 'he'll nae mind fit his ain name is by the time he's feenished wi that lot. And besides if he tries it again, Robbie'll be ridy this time, will ye?'

Robbie nodded grimly, 'aye, he'll nae caal cock me this time, the next time it'll be a fair fecht, and we'll see fit happens then.'

'So Sandy,' said the long-haired student, perhaps sensing that this might be the right time to press home an advantage, 'is it right what the Stot says, that you're looking for other boys to take our jobs?'

Sandy watched as the Stot disappeared round the small stand of alder at the end of the track, 'no boys, I widna go listening to a werd he says, he's jist a druth fa's got the wrang end o the stick. As far as I'm concerned there's nae vacancies on the Summer Crew.'

The Joy Division

SANDY GEDDES, skipper of the Summer Crew, along with the rest of the first boat, walked slowly down the bank holding the top end of the net as Robbie and the Neap rowed the last shot of the first week of the summer salmon netting season. When they'd rowed the coble over to the far bank they turned downstream and rowed hard to the bottom of the pool then back across again. The stingman jumped out then landed and grounded the boat before coming down to help the others haul the net in. After killing the three grilse they caught, the crew, excepting the stingman whose job it was to keep the boat off the river bank with the 20ft long wooden pole they called the sting, slung the tow rope over their shoulders and hauled the boat back up to the bothy by the viaduct.

Half an hour later, with the fish boxed and the bothy and coble locked, Sandy, his first mate, Robbie, and the other two senior members of the crew, Jake and Corbie, stood by the netbox, looking down with some disdain at the three younger, new recruits lying on the grass by the bothy, physically wrecked by their first week's work. The Super, who was due to come up from Tugnet with their pay, was already over ten minutes late and the crew, tired and anxious to get home, had started bickering amongst themselves.

The Neap, whose hands were cut and blistered from a week on the oar opposite Robbie, moaned loudly.

'The loons is feeling a wee bitty sair, by the sounds o things,' said Jake, smiling.

'When I get home, I'm going straight to my bed,' muttered the long-haired student, who had in the course of the first week acquired the nickname Gonzo, because as Robbie said, 'he looks like thon boy fa plays drums in the Muppets.' It had been pointed out to Robbie by both students and the Neap that the drummer in the Muppets was called Animal, but he wouldn't be swayed and the name Gonzo stuck.

'Sandy, faur's the heid-bummer? I'm needin awa,' said Corbie.

'Aye Corbie, I'm needin the same masel, but there's nithing I can dee, the Super'll be here fan he's here,' said the skipper.

'It's typical,' said Corbie bitterly, 'they work us fur the wik and then they treat us like dugs. If we wis in the union, there'd be nane o this hinging aroon waiting fur oor hard earnt pey, if the Super wisna here at five on the dot, we'd be oot on strike.'

'Och, nae wi the union again Corbie, we wint through aa that last year, ye kaen yersel, it nivir ends weel fan we get on te politics,' said Sandy looking unhappy. Corbie scowled and spat on the ground.

*

'Hey Stingman, fit dis it say on yer t-shirt?' asked Robbie, addressing the shorter-haired of the two students by his job title. The Stingman, who was lying with his eyes closed on the grass, didn't answer.

'Oi, Stingman, fit dis it say on yer t-shirt?' repeated Robbie, louder this time.

'Joy Division,' replied the Stingman with his eyes still closed.

'Aye, but fit's that?'

'It's a band.'

'Like rock and roll?'

'Sort of...'

'And ye like this band?'

'Yep, they're good.'

'De ye like em?' Robbie asked Gonzo.

'Nae chance; Joy Division are rubbish,' said Gonzo dismissively.

'No they're not,' said the Stingman, opening his eyes and sitting up to defend the reputation of what he had recently concluded were his fourth favourite band of all time after The Clash at number three and before The Jesus and Mary Chain at number five.

'Oh right,' said Robbie to Gonzo, 'so fit music div ye listen te?'

'Heavy rock, heavy metal.'

'Heavy metal? Fit's that fan it's at hame?' asked Robbie.

'Led Zep, Black Sabbath, AC/DC, that sort of thing.'

Robbie looked nonplussed.

'Thon stuff's ancient,' said the Neap, 'rave music's the thing. Ye've got te move wi the times.'

'Why have you go to move with the times?' said Gonzo heatedly, 'heavy rock is the best..and if you like something and you think it's the best, what's the point in changing just for the sake of it?'

'That's like you wi yer tea, is it Robbie?' said Jake.

'Aye, I suppose so,' said Robbie who'd eaten the same tea since the day when, aged seven, he informed his mother that mince, tatties and peas were his favourite meal and that he wanted it for his tea every night for the rest of his life. His mother, prone to spoiling the young Robbie, whose father had died when his trawler went down off Shetland only a few months after his son was born, didn't refuse the request, reasoning that he would get bored with his new diet soon enough. A fair judgment, but one that proved wide of the mark for, though what Robbie had for his lunch and breakfast varied, forty years later she was still preparing the same tea for the son who'd never moved out. Even when Robbie was in Dr Gray's Hospital for two nights to get his appendix removed, his mother got the bus into Elgin and brought him in his mince, tatties and peas in a Tupperware box, and when she fell and broke her hip a few years later she arranged for Eileen next door to come in and cook Robbie mince, tatties and peas for his tea every night.

'Do you not get bored with mince?' asked the Stingman. Robbie shook his head.

'What about Christmas? What do you do then?'

'I hae a Christmas denner for ma denner, and mince, tatties and peas fur ma tea.'

'It's richt guid mince...' said Sandy, in support of his first mate.

'Oh, so you've hid Robbie's mither's mince, hiv ye...' said Jake, suggestively.

'I've hid it as weel,' said the Neap.

'Fan wis at?' asked Jake, smirking at the students.

'It wis aboot three year ago, fan ma faither took us up te first fit. I hid some then.'

'Mair than some,' muttered Robbie, 'ye hid the hale pan.'

'Wis it guid?' asked Jake.

'Aye, it wis,' said the Neap with a wistful look on his face.

'Fit aboot you, Corbie, hiv you hid Robbie's mither's mince afore?' asked Jake. Corbie nodded.

'Am I the only een in the hale Summer Crew apart fae the students that's nae hid Robbie's mither's mince?' asked Jake feigning indignation and winking at Gonzo, who was trying desperately not to laugh.

'Faur's the Super,' said Corbie angrily, 'I'm needin to get awa.'

Sandy looked at his watch again and hoped that the Super would appear soon.

*

'So fit kind o music is it that Joy Division play?' asked Robbie.

'Have a listen,' said the Stingman pulling his personal stereo from the pocket of his jacket.

As the Stingman rewound the tape Robbie examined the headphones suspiciously, as if they might deliver electro-convulsive therapy or the like, before gingerly putting them on. Having found the right place, the Stingman pressed play, Robbie winced.

'Ye listen to this fur enjoyment?' he said, incredulous. The Stingman nodded.

'Fit's it like?' Jake asked Robbie, after he'd removed the headphones.

'There was a lot a droning in the backgroon and the boy – weel, ye widna cry him a singer – he wis bawling awa, but I've nae idea fit he wis saying, and I've nae idea why they're cried Joy Division, it's the maist depressing thing I've ivir heard in ma life.'

'That's the point; it's ironic,' said the Stingman.

'It's rubbish is fit it is; fit that singer needs is te get oot in the fresh air and dee some herd work, and then he'd feel a bitty better.'

'What, like us?' said Gonzo rubbing his back, ironically.

'Mebbe the boy could dee wi some o Robbie's mither's mince,' said Jake smiling.

'He's dead. Ian Curtis, the lead singer of Joy Division, is dead,' said the Stingman, starting to get annoyed with the lack of respect afforded his fourth favourite band of all time.

'Aye weel, ma mither's mince is guid, but it'll nae bring onybody back fae the deid,' said Robbie. Sandy looked at his watch again and sighed.

'That's it, I've hid enough, fit this country needs is a social-ist revolution to get rid o the toffs and the royals and the bosses; string em aa up,' said Corbie, presumably angered by the fact that the salmon fishing was ultimately owned by one of the richest landowners in Morayshire.

'Corbie, de ye nae think it's a wee bit o an overreaction, winting to get rid o the Queen and young Charlie boy jist because the Super's twenty minutes late wi yer pey,' said Jake, 'and onywey, I thocht you voted nationalist in the last election.'

'I did,' said Corbie defensively, 'I dinna see ony problem wi that. Fit I want is an independent, socialist Scotland.'

'I voted nationalist as weel,' said Robbie, 'but I'm nae a socialist.'

'So you would call yourself a national socialist?' asked the Stingman innocently. Corbie thought for a second.

'Aye, I suppose I wid,' he replied, 'and ye'll see, een o these days we'll be runnin this country.' Jake, annoyed by Corbie's constant moaning, decided to join in on the joke.

'Mebbe you should start yer ain National Socialist perty then,' he said wandering off behind Corbie.

'Mebbe I should, and I tell ye, if I dee then we'll hae oor ane Parliament, and I'll scrap the Poll Tax, hae a better health service, and a tax system that taxes the rich for their property and nae the puir fur their pey...'

'And ye'll be able to sort oot the Super and young Charlie boy,' interrupted Jake, raising his right forefinger to his lip and Seig Heiling with his left as he goose-stepped up and down behind Corbie.

Sandy looked at his watch again and wondered what could be keeping the Super.

*

'O.K then, fit's this hivy stuff like,' said Robbie. Gonzo slipped a tape of AC/DC's *For Those About To Rock* album into the personal stereo and Robbie put on the headphones a second time. After a minute or so Robbie removed them again.

'Och, it's jist the same as the last stuff.'

'What?' said Gonzo, clearly disagreeing with Robbie's judgement. The Stingman shook his head, 'no it's not,' he said, 'it's nothing like it.'

'It is so. I mean the boy's screaming instead o moaning, and it's a wee bitty faster, but it amoonts te the same thing: jist a hale lot o noise…you boys should listen te the King, noo there's some real music…'

'What about you, Sandy, what do you listen to?' asked the Stingman, before Robbie could say anything more on the subject of Elvis.

'It's the traditional stuff fur me – bothy ballads, the Strathspey and Reel, and me and Meg aye tune inte Robbie Sheppard…' And Sandy would have said more, but Jake held his hand up and pointed down to the bottom of the Bridge Pool where an osprey was hanging motionless in the air above the brae. All the crew turned to get a better look as the bird dropped ten feet then hung for an instant before dropping the final forty feet into the shallow fast-flowing water in between the pools. For a moment the bird sat where it landed, looking around as if not sure what to do, then with a couple of flaps of its wings it took off, struggling clear of the water with a shining grilse held tight in its claws, and the Summer Crew were still watching the osprey fly slowly up the river with its catch when the Super pulled into the clearing by the bothy.

'Sorry I'm late boys,' he said, getting out of the pickup, 'but the Bank in Fochabers was on strike, so I hid te ge inte Elgin to get yer pey.'

The Monster

THE STORM RAGED outside the bothy, hurling sheets of rain against the wooden walls, and rattling the cowl on the stove pipe. Inside, however, the bothy was warm and dry, filled with a frowsy heat thrown off by the blazing pot-bellied stove that glowed red in the dim light of the hurricane lamps. Sandy Geddes, skipper of the Summer Crew, had long since concluded there would be no more fishing done that night, however, the crew were compelled to stay on shift, and though they would have all preferred to be at home in their beds, there are worse things in the world than getting paid for sitting around doing nothing in a warm bothy.

Sandy poured himself a generous dram of the broonic that he kept for medical emergencies then looked round the bothy. Jake was catching up with some much-needed sleep on the pile of nets at the back of the bothy. Corbie was trying to fix a broken transistor radio he'd found in a bin in Mosstodloch, and Robbie, the first mate, had just finished a long and rambling tale about his cousin from Auchterless who'd eaten a tin of cat food for a bet. The younger members of the crew were sitting in the battered old armchairs which lined the bothy, stunned by the heat of the pot-bellied stove.

'Sandy, do you mind if I ask you a personal question?' asked the Stingman, wiping a bead of sweat from his brow.

'That depends fit the question is,' said Sandy taking a sip of his whisky.

'How did you lose the tip of the little finger on your left hand?'

Sandy laughed, and looked at his hand, 'och, that's a lang story...'

'Weel, we've got plinty time,' said Robbie looking at his watch, 'as ye said yersel, there's nae mair fushin gan on the nicht.'

'Och, these young loons dinna want to hear aboot ancient history,' said Sandy settling back in his seat.

'No, Sandy go on, tell us,' said the Stingman. Sandy shook his head.

'Aye, go on, tell us,' said the Neap, as he leaned over and placed one of his cheese sandwiches on top of the stove, with the aim of toasting it and melting the cheese at the same time. Sandy looked reluctant, though whether this was genuine reticence or simply part of the storyteller's art is debatable, for thirty seconds later he sat forward in his chair.

'OK, boys I'll tell ye fit happened te ma pinkie,' he said, looking thoughtfully up at the ceiling of the bothy where the flickering light from the open stove and the hurricane lamps played on the roof, 'if ye gan richt back te the beginnin, it wis a nicht like this, aboot…' Sandy stopped and thought once more before turning to the first mate, 'fan wis it Robbie?'

'I wid say it wis aboot five year ago,' said Robbie, looking over at his skipper. Sandy nodded his head then continued.

'Noo ye kaen yersel that a storm efter a lang dry spell freshens the watter and encourages the fush, fa are aa hingin aroon ootside the moo, te enter the river and run up te spawn. Weel, efter that wee spate seven year ago, fan the watter had come back doon a wee bitty, the fush started te run hard. It wis unbelievable, it wis like the aull days, back afore the war, fan there wis that mony fush in the river ye could walk fae ae bank te the ither and nae get yer widers weet…they were running as mony as echt crews in thon days; can ye imagine that boys, echt crews on the river… onywey, faur wis I, Robbie?' asked Sandy having lost the thread a little.

'Ye were saying aboot the strang run five year ago.'

'Oh, aye…in thon twa days efter the spate we landed mair fush than we've taen in the hale o this month so far. They were basically louping in the box and knocking themselves oot, but that's nae the point, the point is that it wis on the final shot o the second day fan I seen it.'

'Seen fit?' asked the Neap leaning over and checking to see how his sandwich was doing.

'The Monster…' said Sandy in a hushed voice, sitting forward in his seat, 'a fifty poon fush. Sitting jist ahind the far pier of the viaduct, resting fae the worse o the current. Ask Robbie, he'll tell ye.'

'Personally, I thocht it was mair like fifty five poon; ony-wey, it wis bigger than Jake,' said Robbie, looking over in the direction of the nets at the back of the bothy.

'Aye,' muttered Jake who had obviously woken up, 'and it wis cleverer than you.'

'Ha, ha,' said Robbie, clearly unamused.

'So what did you do?' asked the Stingman.

'Aye weel, the thing wis there wis nae wey we could actually shoot thon bit o the pool and besides it wis the last shot o the day, so we hid te let it awa,' said Sandy, helping himself to a drop more of the whisky, before sitting back in his seat and continuing with the tale.

'But that nicht though, I couldna stop thinking aboot the monster fush, efter aa there hidna been a fush that size cocht in the river since pre-war days. So the next morning I decided te taak the boat up the river and shoot it doon fae the Pot, up by Fochabers. I mean, ye can nivir really tell hoo far a fush'll run in a nicht; sometimes it's jist up te the next pool and sometimes it could get aa the wey up past the Mulben burn, but there wis something telling me that I hid te get that fish. It wis burning inside me, kaen.'

'He wis like a man possessed,' confirmed Robbie.

'Onywey,' said Sandy, continuing with his tale, 'the next day we shot it doon te the Gow's Island, still catching plinty fush mind, but wi oot ony sign of the monster. Noo, as ye kaen, the Gow's Island pool is a difficult een to work on account o the steep banks and the deep, fast flowing watter, but as soon as we started te haal the net we kaent we hid a big bag, even in spite o the strang current, but it was only fan we hid the net hauf in, that the Monster breached.'

'Aye, Sandy,' said Robbie, 'you near let go o the net you

wis that excited.'

'Aye, I wis sure we hid it.'

'So fit happened?' asked the Neap turning the sandwich which had filled the bothy with the pleasant smell of toasting bread and melting cheese.

'You've seen a fush loup oer the net afore, hiv ye?' The younger members of the Summer Crew, who were by now all sitting forward in their seats listening attentively, nodded their heads.

'And ye can tell it's jist luck, they jist jump kaen. Nae this time…I swear the Monster kaent exactly fit it wis deein. It wis like it hung in the air and looked at me wi its een guid ee, then dipped its heid oer the tap o the net and it wis awa…the salmon is an amazing fush.'

'What do you mean, "it's one good eye"?' asked Gonzo.

'Jist fit I said. The other ee wis missing, tain oot by a seal or an otter, or fit ivir.'

'It wis unreal,' said Robbie shaking his head.

'OK, but that doesn't explain how you lost your little finger,' said the Stingman.

'Aye weel, if ye ca canny, I'll tell ye,' said Sandy leaning over and pouring himself more whisky before picking up the narrative where he left off.

'OK, so that wikend I took ma wife, Meg, oer te see her sister in Inverurie, but aa the wey there and aa the wey back I couldna think o onything else but that fush and the wey it stared at me as it louped the net.'

'It et ye up, did it, Sandy?'

'Ye could say that, Robbie,' said Sandy nodding his head in agreement, before continuing with his tale. 'The next three days we shot doon the river. Well, ye kaen yersel, ye'll nae get mony complaints aboot that fae the crew, efter aa there's nae haaling te be deen and ye get a good change o scene, but the rods dinna like it and there wis a complaint sent fae the Association and fae the Laird.'

'So what did you do?' asked the Stingman.

'I pretended I'd nae seen it and loaded her up for ae last go…onywey, te cut a lang story short, we wis haaling in on the Pot on the final day, fan the Monster breached for a second time, but this time I wis ridy. I hid twa o the boys in the watter to lift the corks and this time it werked, the fush couldna get oot. It tried mind, twice. But it couldna. Onywey, we haaled the net up onta the scap, wi the Monster in the bug and I leaned doon te steady the Monster to skelp it on the heid wi ma priest, fan it suddenly turnt on me, and sunk its teeth into the pinkie o ma left haun.'

Sandy held his hand aloft, waggling his truncated pinkie in the flickering light of the hurricane lamps, 'it bit it right off, richt through the bone.'

'But you got the fish?' asked the Stingman.

'Na,' said Sandy shaking his head sadly, 'because wi a flick o its tail it was aff the scap and inta the shallows and afore ony o us could react, it wis awa again…like snaw aff a o dyke. I would have sworn it kaent exactly fit it wis deen.'

'Aye, the salmon is an amazing fush,' said Robbie echoing Sandy's earlier observation, 'thon fush wis born the size o Sandy's pinkie in a burn up the strath some wey, and look at it noo.'

'Fan ye think aboot fit it hid te go through te get to thon size, it maaks the mind boggle,' said Sandy nodding in agreement.

'So fit happened te the monster?' asked the Neap.

'It was last seen heading doon the river again,' said Robbie.

'Chawing on Sandy's pinkie,' said Jake, sitting up on the pile of nets and stretching. Everyone laughed as Jake sniffed the air.

'Fit's that smell,' he asked, wincing.

'Oh no, ma piece, its ruined,' wailed the Neap spotting his by now badly burned cheese sandwich smouldering on the stove top.

*

The Atlantic salmon is, as both Sandy and Robbie observed, a remarkable fish. Its life cycle is one of the great wonders of the natural world, taking it on a journey from its birthplace in the small burns high up in the hills to the frozen seas off Greenland and Iceland and back again. During the course of this epic journey it has to swim and navigate thousands of miles; completely change its body chemistry twice as it moves from fresh to salt water and back again; avoid being eaten by seals, orca and a host of other predators; scale waterfalls, run rapids and of course avoid the attentions of fishermen of all stripes. Those fish that overcome these obstacles and make it back to spawn and die in their native burn are only a small fraction of those that leave. However, what is perhaps most remarkable is that not all these fish die after their epic journey; some, a small fraction of a small fraction, survive spawning and make the journey one, two or even three more times. The monster was one such fish; a fraction of who knows how many fractions, an anomaly, an outlier, a white stag or a black swan. And it was this that obsessed Sandy, for he knew how rare and remarkable a thing it was. And it stirred in him an inexplicable desire to catch it; to possess it. A desire beyond reason that haunts the hearts of many of us in one way or another.

That a man might become obsessed with a fish may seem a little peculiar to those who have had little do with fish or fishing, however, Sandy's obsession, while possibly a little more developed than most, was and is not unusual, for the Atlantic salmon is one of the very few fish that seems capable of provoking strong emotion in us. Quite why people should develop such deep feelings for the Atlantic salmon and not for the saithe, gurnard or tench can only be a matter of conjecture, but perhaps it has something to do with the fact that we see in the lifecycle of the Atlantic salmon a parallel of our own trials and tribulations as we journey through life. Or maybe it's down to the way it looks: a fresh-run grilse that shimmers silver with all the colours of the rainbow is a particularly handsome thing that seems to be possessed of an innate nobility that the haddock, for example, lacks. But maybe it's neither metaphor nor aesthetic that attracts us; maybe it's just because it tastes nice. Who knows? What is certain, however, is that Sandy is by no means the only person to become obsessed with the Atlantic salmon.

*

Two days after the storm, Sandy was sitting outside the bothy after a shot, relaxing in the wan sun and smoking his pipe, when the two students came running down from the viaduct.

'Sandy, Sandy, we've just seen the monster,' said the Stingman breathlessly. Sandy stood up, then sat back down again.

'Aye, aye boys, ye almost hid me there, but I'm nae that feil,' he said, nonchalantly slipping his pipe back into his mouth.

'No, no, Sandy,' said Gonzo, 'come and see, I swear if we're lying, you can gie us oor jotters.'

Up on the viaduct, Sandy and Robbie lay looking down through the metal slats to the water below. It was Robbie who spoke first.

'That's it skip. See its ee? It's missing...' Sandy said nothing, but lay there watching the monster which, to quote Herman Melville, that great chronicler of marine biological obsession,

> 'swam before him as the monomaniac incarnation
> of all those malicious agencies...all that most mad-
> dens and torments; all that stirs up the lees of
> things; all truth with malice in it; all that cracks the
> sinews and cakes the brain...'

'Fit are we g'te dee, skip?' asked Robbie.

'We're g'te shoot under the brig. I'm nae letting him get awa this time,' said Sandy calmly determined.

'No, skip, ye canna, the current's oer strang and there's the rocks fae the railway line, ye'll get the gear snagged.'

But Sandy wasn't listening. He stood up and brushed himself down and he was just about to turn back towards the bothy when something fell from his pocket, clattering noisily before falling through one of the slats in the iron bridge and into the dark water below.

'Fit wis that?' asked Robbie.

'Ma lighter.'

'The een yer niece gave ye?'

'Aye...it's nae disturbed the fush, his it?' asked Sandy apparently unconcerned by the loss of this prized possession.

'No, it's still faur it wis,' said the Neap, who was still lying down watching the fish. The Neap was left stationed on the viaduct to keep an eye on the fish while the rest of the crew got ready.

'Sandy, are ye sure…' said Robbie.

'Robbie, fa's skipper o this crew?' said Sandy with a fixed look on his face.

Salmon fishers always shoot a pool from the top, making best use of the current, however in their attempt to catch the monster, Robbie and Jake had to row under the bridge and against the current as it wasn't possible to launch a boat from the top of the pool on the other side, so it was with no little skill and effort that Robbie and Jake managed to get the boat in place so that Sandy could lay the net between the monster and the stone pier without scaring it unduly. When they landed the net everyone was quiet, concentrating on the job at hand. When the net was halfway in, the water suddenly exploded and the monster breached, but the Neap and Gonzo were on hand to lift the corks, thwarting its attempted escape.

'We've got the Monster this time,' said Robbie, excitedly, but when they got the net onto the scap there was no sign of the great fish which had escaped through a large hole ripped in the net by the large, jagged rocks used for the railway line embankment.

When the rest of the crew left that night, Sandy locked the bothy and walked over to the bank of the river, where he stood for a long while looking into the dark brooding water running under the bridge. The great fish had eluded him once more.

The Blank Day

WHEN SANDY GEDDES, skipper of the Summer Crew, arrived for the early afternoon start of the back shift he was surprised to find the patch of grass outside the bothy occupied by a group of middle-aged men and women, sitting at easels, painting the view of the river and the old railway viaduct. And he was about to ask them to move when he spotted the tall, thin, grey-haired figure of the Revd. Alistair Michie striding towards him.

'Sandy, how are you?' asked the Revd. Michie cheerfully.

'Oh, hullo Minister, I didn't see you there.'

'Oh no Sandy, it's not Minister anymore, it's just plain old mister; I've given up my role as a "fisher of men",' said the no longer Revd. Alistair Michie smiling at his own joke. Sandy nodded his head and looked over at the painters. The erstwhile Reverend followed his gaze.

'I hope you don't mind the Art Group; we're not in your

way, are we?'

'Er, well,' said Sandy, reaching into his pocket and retrieving his pipe as he considered how best to tell the Revd. Michie that they were indeed right, slap-bang in the way.

'It's just that I had dinner with the Laird's wife a couple of weeks ago, and she said it wouldn't be a problem…'

'Er, O.K….' said Sandy, putting the pipe back in his pocket, 'I'm sure that will be fine.'

'Jolly good, Sandy,' said the Revd. Michie clapping his hands, 'it's nice to know that the salmon fishers are supporters of the arts.'

*

'Fit right dis thon pompous gowk hae te tell us fit te dee and fit nae te dee,' said Corbie spitting on the ground.

'Och noo, calm doon Corbie, that's a man o God yer spikkin aboot,' said Jake.

'Nae ony mair,' said Sandy.

'Aye, fit wis he saying aboot him being a fisherman? He's nae thinking aboot jining the crew is he?' asked Robbie, who had never paid much attention at Sunday school.

'No,' said Sandy shaking his head, 'fit he wis saying, in a roon aboot kinda wey, is that he's nae a minister ony mair. He's lost his faith.'

'He should look doon the back o the sofa,' said Jake, smiling, 'fan I lose ma keys, that's faur I aye find em.'

'Are ye saying he's an atheist?' asked Robbie, thoughtfully. Sandy nodded, 'Aye that's aboot it.'

'I'm an atheist,' said the Stingman, proudly.

'Fit kind o atheist?' asked Corbie.

'What do you mean?'

'Are you a Protestant atheist, or a Catholic atheist?'

'Look boys, that's enough, we dinna want to get inte aa that, let's jist maak the best of the situation,' said Sandy, keen to avoid any discussion of sectarian matters, that experience told him never ended well. However, the rest of the Summer Crew were unhappy about the imposition, and made it clear with a series of disgruntled asides.

'If he disna believe in God ony mair, dis he aye taak his pension fae the kirk?' asked Jake loudly, as they walked down to the river to start the first shot.

*

The Summer Crew worked around the Art Group as best they could, though, as a consequence of the recent hot, dry weather there were so few fish in the river that the first three shots were blank, which in turn meant there was no great urgency to the work, and therefore little inconvenience.

As the Summer Crew were hauling in the fourth shot of the day, the Revd. Michie left the Art Group to their own devices, and came to watch.

'Caught many today?' he asked. Sandy looked up from where he was hauling the net and shook his head.

'Not a thing.'

'We could be deeing wi the help o yer boss here the day, minister,' said Jake looking skyward, as he piled the net on the scap. The Revd. Michie smiled awkwardly but said nothing.

'It's the water, it's awful low. We've been praying for rain for a week now,' said Sandy intervening hastily, then remembering who he was speaking to, 'sorry, minister, I didn't mean to erm…'

'Look Sandy, I told you, I'm done with all of that…' said the Revd. Michie, sounding a little strained, 'in fact, I've just published a short monograph entitled "*The Pointlessness of Prayer*"'

'Are ye saying that it's nae g'te rain?' asked Jake, smiling at the Revd. Michie who paused briefly before looking up at the cloudless sky.

'Yes, I suppose I am,' he said, smiling back at Jake, 'look,' he continued, looking down at the net, 'I think you've got a fish.' And sure enough, the net had a ten pound grilse in it. Unfortunately, however, the fish had two lampreys attached to its belly; their broad, mottled tails writhing around on the hot stones of the scap.

'I hate hagfush,' said Corbie, hitting the already half-dead grilse on the head with the short stick that all salmon fishers carry for dispatching fish, and which is, presumably ironically, called the priest as it administers the last rights.

'I canna understand why they exist at aa. I mean, fit's the point o hagfush? They're jist parasites, sooking the guts oot o a nice clean fish like that.'

'Indeed, the existence of evil in this world is the rock upon which the fragile barque of my own faith foundered,' said the Revd. Michie thoughtfully, before quickly looking away as Corbie cut the lampreys from the fish and ground them into the scap with the heel of his wader. Once he was satisfied that the lampreys were dead Corbie picked up the grilse by the knuckle and tossed it back into the water where it spun slowly out into the current, then off downstream.

The clear, pleasant heat of the morning curdled into a sultry, airless late afternoon and at about five o'clock a large bank of convectional cloud bubbled up from behind Ben Aigan and drifted down the river toward the coast. Thunder rolled around the hazy sky. And still the Summer Crew had caught nothing they could box.

'Robbie, if things dinna change this'll be the first time since I jined the fishing, thirty year ago, that we hivna cocht a single boxable fish in a day.'

'Aye, I kaen,' said Robbie shaking his head, 'we've nae even hid a finnock or a yaldie. It's nae guid. We could be looking at a blank day.' The words were enough to send a shiver down Sandy's spine.

'It's thon defrocked vicar, he's brocht bad luck wi him. He's a Jonah,' said Robbie looking up at the Revd. Michie who was mopping his brow as he stood supervising the Art Group in the full glare of the sun.

Fishermen, like many of those who depend directly on fate for their livelihood, are extremely superstitious, and there are a range of circumstances, objects and people that, in their eyes, can spell disaster for a crew, boat, or catch. Things as diverse and unlikely as mentioning rabbits on board, eating bananas, or meeting a member of the clergy on the way to the boat (ditto redheads and any flat-footed person).

'Aye weel, Robbie, that's as mebbe, but it's probably got mair te dee wi the oer fushing in the North Atlantic feeding grounds, the pollution and the low watter,' said Sandy, who was, at heart, a rationalist, 'ye kaen the catches hiv bin getting werse and werse ivry year.'

'Either wey it's nae guid,' said Robbie looking at the Revd. Michie who was peering at the easel of one of the members of the Art Group.

'Fit happens if the catches keep drapping?' asked Corbie, 'fit'll happen te us?'

'We'll be on the broo like Mr Michie oer there,' said Jake glumly.

*

At around half past five, as the Summer Crew were sitting down to their tea, the Revd. Michie clapped his hands together, 'OK, OK,' he said in a loud voice, 'it's just about time to pack up, but before we do, I want everyone to gather round here and look at Ginny's work, which I think is the pick of the catch, as it were.'

The Art Group, and behind them the Summer Crew, gathered round a rather embarrassed looking middle-aged woman wearing a blue fisherman's smock and brightly coloured tie-dyed cotton trousers and a pair of Birkenstock sandals.

'Now, see how Ginny's bravura use of chiaroscuro elevates the subject above the mere mimetic, beyond the nature of the viaduct *qua* bridge...' said the Revd. Michie, standing back from the picture slightly and sweeping his hands across the painting with an expansive gesture.

'She's caught the Neap weel,' said Jake, *sotto voce*, 'see the wey his moo's hinging open, and his hauns is in his pooches, that's spot on.'

'...and embued it with a moral and didactic quality that is the essence of all great art.'

'Fit's the minister blethering aboot noo?' asked Robbie.

'I think he's suggesting that the viaduct is a metaphor...' whispered the Stingman and he would have said more had it not suddenly started raining heavily sending the Art Group scurrying off to their cars clutching rain-splashed watercolours and leaving the Summer Crew in peace to catch the fish which started to run later that evening in response to either the absence of the Revd. Michie or the fresh water in the river, depending upon whether you believed Sandy or Robbie. Either way, Sandy avoided the blank day that he so dreaded.

Jock Stewart's Big Walk Round Scotland

SANDY GEDDES, skipper of the Summer Crew, and his first mate, Robbie, were leaning on the netbox, watching a pair of mergansers fly low up the river when the Super pulled up in the pickup to collect the fish.

'Fit wis the catch the day?' asked the Super as he got out of the pickup.

'Nae great te be honest, though we've been trying wer herdest; wi deen echt shots afore we even hid wer piece,' said Sandy as the Super tallied the fish.

'OK, dinna hash yersel oer mich, it is fit it is, naebidy's catching onything at the moment – the rods or the permanent crew,' said the Super as Robbie loaded the boxes onto the back of the pickup. Sandy nodded his head and sighed despondently, and the Super was just about to get back into the pickup, when he stopped and turned.

'Well, here's something that'll mebbe cheer ye up – we've got a visitor coming at the end o the wik.'

'Oh aye, fa's that?' asked Sandy.

'Jock Stewart.'

'Fa's he?'

'Nae thon boy fae off the telly?' said Robbie with some excitement. The Super nodded.

'Fit boy?' asked Sandy who didn't watch TV, and whose only knowledge of television personalities was that his wife and her mother had it in for someone called Barlow, who they both thought had 'ideas above his station.'

'Kaen, that boy fit dis the tours roon Scotland…' said Robbie, who watched a lot of TV with his mother.

'That's the cheil,' said the Super, 'he deen *Jock Stewart's Mountains* then *Jock Stewart's Islands* and now he's deein anither een fa he's walking richt roond the country, it's g'te be cried *Jock Stewart's Big Walk Round Scotland.*'

*

The salmon fishers were used to an audience: there were often a couple of dog walkers or rod fishers watching them work the river, but they never let that affect the way they dressed, however, it was a remarkably smart looking Summer Crew that turned up on the day of Jock Stewart's visit. Sandy was wearing his best pair of waders, Robbie had run a comb through his hair, and even Corbie had gone so far as to wash his neck. The only disappointment was the students.

'Look, at ye,' said Robbie, 'ye look like a pair of wild tinks fae the Belts.'

'We're keeping it real,' said Gonzo who had back-combed his long mane of hair for the occasion, while the Stingman had put on his new Public Enemy t-shirt especially.

Robbie was about to say more when a long-wheelbase Land Rover, towing a large, expensive-looking caravan lumbered up the track from the main road.

The driver of the Land Rover, a slightly harassed looking middle-aged woman wearing an open-collared cambric shirt, wound down the window.

'Is this the salmon fishery?' she asked in a rather refined Edinburgh accent, as she fished a pair of small, stylish reading glasses with multi-coloured frames out of the pocket of her shirt and perched them on the end of her nose.

'That's right,' said Robbie.

'My name's Catriona, I'm the director of *Jock Stewart's Big Walk Round Scotland*, can I speak to err…Sandy, please,' she said casting an eye over the production notes lying on the dashboard.

'That's me,' said Sandy stepping forward.

'Excellent, excellent,' said the director opening the door, and sizing Sandy up with the small lens that hung on a silver chain around her neck.

'OK, team let's get set up,' she said, turning to the film crew sitting in the back of the Land Rover.

'Where's Jock?' asked Robbie as the film crew unloaded their gear and started setting up.

'Err, he's still in bed,' said the director looking round at the caravan, 'he's feeling a little under the weather. It's this flu that's going round.'

'I thocht he wis supposed te be walkin the length o Scotland, hoo could he be deeing that if he got a lift here in the caravan?' asked Corbie to Jake as the director walked off to supervise the crew.

'The boy's ill, Corbie,' said Jake smiling, 'he's got the flu that's gan aroon.'

'Fit flu is that?'

'It mist be the een he cocht in the bar of the Germouth Hotel last nicht – he wis in there til three o'clock fae fit Sylvia Main telt me fan I wis picking up ma paper this morning,' said Corbie with a frown.

Catriona, the director, took Sandy to one side as the film crew set up.

'There's just a couple of things I want to go through while Jock gets prepared...' she said in a slightly apologetic manner. Sandy nodded.

'OK, first, he doesn't really like people looking him directly in the eye. Now, I know it's a little difficult to get used to, but he gets a lot of attention, so it would be good if you could ask your men not to look directly at him.' Sandy nodded, but said nothing, unsure of what to make of the director's request.

'Also, second, we're going to have to get rid of those two,' said the director pointing to the Stingman and Gonzo, 'we want to keep this as authentic as possible.'

'Well, they're part o the crew,' said Sandy hesitantly, 'I mean, he works the sting.'

'Look Sandy,' said Catriona taking off her glasses, massaging the bridge of her nose, then looking at him directly, 'I don't mean to be obtuse, but our viewers expect a certain type of thing from Jock's programmes. And that,' she said, pointing at the two students, 'is not it.' As Sandy pondered how best to break the news to the students, a middle-aged man wearing a purple shell suit and white trainers stuck his head out of the caravan.

'Catriona,' he shouted, 'where's ma lighter, who's seen ma fucking lighter?' Catriona rolled her eyes.

'Don't worry Jock. I'm coming. I'm coming.'

*

'What do you mean we're not authentic. We're authentic as it comes,' said the Stingman indignantly.

'Boys, I'm sorry, but there's nithing I can dee. It's fur the TV.'

'We're keeping it real,' said Gonzo.

'She disna wint that.'

'You could stand up for us on principle,' said the Stingman.

'Aye, but she said she widna dee it if you were in it. She said there wis plinty ither things she could film, and that they'd jist ging up te Baxters and film there if we didna dee fit she asked.'

'What, to film soup being made?' asked the Stingman.

'It widna suprise me; fowk'll watch onything on the TV,' said Corbie, who had a low opinion of the medium.

'My mither and her pals wid watch programmes aboot soup aa day lang, particularly if they wis presented by Jock,' said Robbie.

'Aye, weel they better nae film the quines on the beetroot line fan they're up there or they'll be broadcasting stuff that wid maak even Jock blush,' chipped in Jake.

'Onywey, that's aa irrelevant; the point is that we're nae missing oor chance to be on the telly jist because you twa nivir made the effort te pit on daecent claithes,' said Robbie emphatically, and Gonzo was just about to reply when the caravan door opened and Jock Stewart stepped out.

A miraculous change had come over the portly television presenter. Gone were the purple shell suit and trainers, replaced by a brightly-coloured voluminous kilt, an over-sized fur sporran fashioned from the pelt of what appeared to be several dead animals, and a white puffy shirt with a lace-up collar such as pirates used to wear. To top the look off he wore a pair of highly-polished hobnail boots and in his hand he carried a large and intricately carved shepherd's crook.

'Wid ye look at thon sark...' said Corbie with some amazement.

'Noo, there's an authentic Scotsman fur you,' said Jake smiling at the students.

*

'Sandy, Sandy, Sandy, my auld friend, hoo are ye?' asked Jock, striding over to where Sandy stood mending a net.

'Very well, Jock,' said Sandy, a little awkwardly.

'Hoo lang has it been, Sandy?' asked Jock, slipping his arms out of the straps of the small canvas knapsack he was carrying, and leaning on his shepherd's crook.

'Sorry,' said Sandy, looking perplexed.

'Since we last met...look, Catriona, has he no been briefed,' said Jock angrily, as he turned to the director. Catriona filled Sandy in as Jock walked back to his mark.

'Sorry Sandy,' she said, 'one of the conventions we follow is that Jock is an old friend of all the people he meets. It helps the folks at home to feel more comfortable with the format. You know, they all believe that Jock is their friend so, of course, any friend of Jock must, by extension, be a friend of theirs.'

'So Sandy, Sandy, Sandy, hoo lang has it been?' asked Jock a second time.

'A long time,' replied Sandy uncertainly.

'Aye weel Sandy, it's richt guid to see you again, de ye mind the capers we used tae hae…' said Jock wrapping his arm round Sandy and grinning broadly at the camera.

'Cut,' shouted the director.

'What is it this time?' asked an enraged Jock, 'that was fine for me.' The director pointed to the river bank behind the two men where the Stingman and Gonzo had some-how accidentally managed to wander into shot.

'Jock, we'll take it from your piece to camera…' said the director after the students had been moved away and severely warned about further encroachment.

'This is my auld friend, Sandy Geddes, captain of the salmon boats on the River Spey. It was Sandy that taught "wee Jocky Stewart" all he knows about the salmon. Isn't that right Sandy?' said Jock wrapping his arm round Sandy again.

'Aye, that's right, Jock,' said Sandy, slightly confused by the presenter's detour into the third person.

'Aye, Sandy,' said Jock suddenly breaking into song,

> 'For we twa hae run aboot the braes,
> and pou'd the gowans fine,
> but we've wander'd monie a weary fit,
> sin auld lang syne.'

'O.K, cut there. That's perfect, Jock, perfect,' said the director when Jock had finished singing, 'now let's get the boys in the boats and get some of the action shots.' As the film crew moved their camera equipment down onto the scap Jock reached into his sporran and pulled out a packet of Superkings, lit one then offered the packet to Sandy. Sandy shook his head and pulled out his pipe.

'Look Sandy, ye don't know if there's a massage parlour around here do ye? In Elgin or something? I need a good rub doon, if ye know whit ah mean,' said Jock winking at Sandy.

'Mebbe, but I widna really kaen,' replied Sandy thoughtfully, 'but ye could aye nip inta the Doctor's Surgery in Fochabers, if it's a bad back that ye've got.' Jock seemed nonplussed by the idea.

'So where are you off te next?' asked Sandy trying to keep the conversation alive.

'We're aff to a distillery tonight; get swallied,' said Jock rubbing his hands together, 'then back tae Marbella.'

'Oh, are you off on a holiday?' asked Sandy.

'No, no, I live there. Get away fae this manky weather. It's very "tax efficient" as well; know what I mean? Actually, if you're interested in moving out there, I've got a thing going with these Russian guys who run a timeshare complex…it's a great deal…only thirty miles fae the sea,' said Jock rummaging in his sporran and handing Sandy a business card he found there.

*

The salmon crew, minus the students, spent the rest of the afternoon rowing up and down the river to satisfy the demands of Jock and the director, and by the time they were finished they were all thoroughly disenchanted with the process of filmmaking. However, their spirits lifted when they returned to the bothy where they discovered the two students sitting on fishboxes drinking beer and reading magazines on the grass in front of the bothy.

'Have a drink and a jazz mag boys,' said Gonzo, pointing to two cases of beer and a bottle of whisky standing next to the large pile of glossy magazines.

'What on earth…' said Jock. Jake walked over and picked up one of the magazines.

'Oh, my god, will ye taak look at her, she's nae shy,' he said, picking up the magazine on top of the pile and show-ing it to the rest of the crew.

'Her mither mist be richt proud o her…' said Robbie, shaking his head.

'Faur aboots did ye get aa this fae?' asked Sandy.

'The mobile lending library,' said Gonzo, pointing at Jock Stewart's caravan. Jock turned red and started spluttering.

'Aye, it's not a walking tour of Scotland that he's on…' said the Stingman, emphasising the verb, however, before he could continue, he was interrupted by Sandy.

'Look boys, gie Jock back his, er…reading material.'

'They're no mine, they're nothing to do with me,' said Jock hastily.

'Jock, what do you think of her?' asked Gonzo, holding up the magazine he was reading, but Jock had already disap-peared into his caravan.

*

When *Jock Stewart's Big Walk Round Scotland* aired in the New Year there was no mention of his visit to the salmon fishery at the mouth of the Spey, or of his old friend Sandy

Geddes, with whom he'd 'pou'd the gowans fine' and who had taught him all he knew about the salmon, and it was no consolation to Robbie that the hastily shot section on the making of Baxter's Cock-a-Leekie soup that replaced the Summer Crew on the programme was, as he had predicted, very well received by his mother and her friends.

The Sikoda

SANDY GEDDES, the skipper of the Summer Crew, was running late for work, and by the time he arrived for the start of the shift the rest of the crew were sheltering in the bothy from the light rain that had been falling for the last hour or so. As Sandy drew up he noticed, parked by the bothy, a car he had not seen before.

'Fa's car's that oot ben?' asked Sandy, as he settled into the large, battered armchair at the end of the bothy and began to fill his first pipe of the day. Jake, who was reading a copy of Exchange and Mart, looked up and smiled.

'That's ma new Sikoda,' said Robbie, the first mate, with evident pride, 'I decided te get rid o the motorbike.'

'Sorry, fit maak is it?' asked Sandy, lighting his pipe, looking perplexed.

'A 1.2 litre Sikoda Estelle,' replied Robbie, repeating the addition of the extraneous letter in the car's name.

'Thon Sikodas is richt guid cars,' said Jake, winking at Sandy who was about to reply when he was startled by a loud groan emanating from the pile of nets behind him in the corner of the bothy, where, when he turned round to look, he spotted the prostrate form of Gonzo. 'Fit's awrang wi him?' asked Sandy.

'He wis at a perty last night,' explained the Neap in between bites of a fish paste sandwich his mother had made him for his lunch.

'Wis he bad?'

'Like a cowpit yow, but that's nae the werst o it – he wis aff wi a quine fae Portgordon,' said the Neap starting on a second sandwich.

'So, yer shagged oot. Is that it?' said Robbie, kicking the pile of nets and causing Gonzo to groan once more. 'Weel, fit dee ye expect if will hang aroond wi loose wumen.'

'Och, leave the pair loon alane,' said Jake, 'you'd gie onything te get thon young quiney in the back of your Sikoda.'

'That's rubbish, I dinna go chasing efter young quines,' said Robbie, hotly denying the accusation.

'Aye, Robbie's happy enough if they've got aa their ane teeth and their tattoos are spelt richt,' said the Neap, wiping a small constellation of crumbs from the front of his t-shirt.

'OK, OK, enough of this nonsense boys,' said Sandy, struggling to his feet, 'it's time we got te werk.'

'Aw no, Sandy, it's raining,' complained Gonzo, 'can we nae hae another half hour?' A petition that found considerable support among the other members of the crew.

'Typical student, jist idle, bone idle,' said Robbie with disgust, kicking the nets again, an act which this time caused Gonzo to sit bolt upright.

'Robbie, what would you say if I told you I could double the value of your car in less than two minutes?' said Gonzo, rubbing his eyes.

'Fit de you mean?' said Robbie suspiciously.

'I can double the value of the car in less than two minutes, if you give me the keys.'

'I'm nae gieing onybody the keys to ma new car, especially the likes o you. Fa kaens fit diseases you've got.'

'Hey Robbie, he's g'te double the value o yer car. Ye canna turn that doon,' said Jake, sensing there might be some fun to be had at Robbie's expense.

'I promise I won't damage the car in any way,' said Gonzo.

'Jist tell us fit yer g'te dee and then I'll dee it masel,' said Robbie.

'Sorry,' said Gonzo, shaking his head, 'it's too difficult to explain, I can only do it by showing you.'

Despite his reservations, a mixture of greed and curiosity got the better of Robbie. The rain, which had so recently rendered work an impossibility, was forgotten as the members of the Summer Crew crowded round Robbie's new car to see exactly what Gonzo would do.

'If onything happens te that car, I'll maak sure ye'll pey for it,' said Robbie menacingly as he handed Gonzo the keys.

'Aye, aye dinna worry,' said Gonzo, opening the door before calmly reaching into his pocket, pulling out a fifty pence piece and placing it on the dashboard.

'There you are; now it's worth a whole pound,' he said, closing the door and handing the keys back to Robbie.

When the hilarity had subsided a little, Sandy intervened.

'Noo, noo, come on boys, this is neither catching fish nor mending nets,' he said, tapping out his pipe on the side of the bothy, 'let's hae a wee shotty o the Brig Pool.'

In fact, they shot the Bridge Pool and then carried on down to shoot the Lower Bridge Pool as well, catching twelve grilse and a fine, fresh-run, nineteen pound cock salmon in the process, then, after the long haul back up the river bank, and having boxed the fish, Robbie's new car became, once more, the subject of their attention.

'Robbie, that right front wing – it's a gey roch looking paint job on it,' said Jake.

'Och aye, that,' said Robbie, scratching a nasty looking horsefly bite on his arm, 'weel, that's pairt of the reason I got the car so chape. The boy fa owned it afore – he's a brasher in the wid up by Knockando – onywey, he wis gan te work ae morning fan he hit a roe deer. It was back aboot twa wiks ago, kaen, fan it wis gey misty; he didna see it coming.'

'He saw you coming, though,' observed Jake.

'Fit's that supposed to mean?' asked Robbie sharply.

'Oh nithing, nithing,' said Jake, examining the toes of his waders.

'Weel, ye can think fit ye like, but I kaen I got myself a richt bargain. The boy even threw in a haunch o the deer fur free.'

'So wis it the brasher that did the paint job on the dent?' asked the Neap, peeling the silver foil off a Tunnock's tea cake.

'No, that wis me,' said Robbie with some pride.

'Fit did ye use, emulsion or something?' continued the Neap.

'Weel nae quite, I mean I wis g'te buy some o thon car paint, but it wis gey expensive and I realised I hid a wee suppy gloss left fae decorating the skirting in ma mither's hoose last year; it was a near perfect match.'

*

Despite the rest of the Summer Crew's scepticism, the Skoda was a great boon to Robbie, who had never owned a car before, and over the next few evenings it propelled him as far as Deveronside to the east and the banks of the River Findhorn to the west, breaking down only once in the course of his travels and, fortunately for Robbie, that was only a few hundred yards from the garage at Alves. However, Robbie's enjoyment of this new found freedom was marred somewhat by Gonzo who had been tormenting him all week with a seemingly unending stream of Skoda jokes.

'I say, I say, I say, what do you call a Sikoda with a sun roof?' asked Gonzo, immitating the manner of a music hall comedian. Robbie ignored him.

'I don't know, Gonzo, what do you call a Sikoda with a sun roof?' replied the Stingman, who had adopted the role of straight man in what was a blossoming comic double act.

'A skip,' came the reply.

By the Thursday of the shift, however, the senior fishers, Jake included, found this brand of humour beginning to grate and that lunch time Sandy amended the unofficial constitution of the Summer Crew and introduced, with immediate effect, a ban on all Skoda jokes, widening the prohibition half way through the afternoon to include all derogatory or humorous references to any make of Eastern European car.

Despite the ban, Robbie was still smarting from the

ill-treatment he had suffered at the hands of the students, and on his divagations around the North-East, he racked his brain for a way to get back at them. As it turned out, Robbie didn't have to wait long before providence smiled on him once more when, that Saturday, on a drive round Ordiequish and the Teindland, he made a brief stop at a jumble sale in the village hall at Inchberry where, next to a jigsaw of the Sydney Opera House (some missing pieces), he discovered the instrument of his revenge.

*

The next week found the Summer Crew on the night shift which ran from ten in the evening 'til six the following morning. On the Monday, after the first couple of shots, Gonzo, the Stingman, and the Neap were sat in the Neap's car listening to the radio. Robbie took the opportunity to show Sandy, Jake and Corbie his Inchberry purchase.

'Fit is that? It's clear like varnish or something...' said Sandy stirring the stick round the pot of paint that Robbie had produced from the boot of his car.

'O.K, but jist stay faur ye are, while I blow oot the lamps.'

'Fit are ye talking aboot,' said Corbie, indignantly.

'You'll see. You'll see,' replied Robbie leaning over and extinguishing the two hurricane lamps which lit the bothy. However, instead of being plunged into darkness as Sandy, Jake and Corbie had expected, the bothy remained lit by an ethereal glow radiating from the tin of paint Robbie had bought at Inchberry.

'Oh, my god Robbie fit on earth is that ye've got?' asked Sandy.

'Luminescent paint.'

'Fit?'

'It's glow in the dark, kaen, like they use fur the watches.'

'And fit exactly are ye g'te dee wi that?' asked Jake.

Robbie outlined his plan as he relit the hurricane lamps, concluding that, 'aa we need is een o thon black bin bags and we're cooking by gas.'

*

The Friday of a night shift was usually disliked by the younger members of the Summer Crew who feared that they were missing out on some of the fun enjoyed by friends and compatriots in the local public houses and nightclubs, so it wasn't unusual for the skipper to compensate and motivate his crew on a Friday night shift with a crate of beer purchased from the local hotel with a silver currency dragged from the river and beaten insensate on the first shot of the night.

And so it was that Friday, when Sandy sent Gonzo and the Stingman over to the hotel for a crate of Export. As soon as they had disappeared over the viaduct, Robbie put his plan into action.

About an hour and a half later Gonzo and the Stingman reappeared, both in a state of some agitation.

'Fit's awrang boys?' asked Jake, deadpan, 'ye look like ye've seen aull Nick himsel.'

'I think we have…I mean, we've jist seen something on that bridge, I don't know what it was, but it was…uncanny,' said Gonzo, sitting down, his hands shaking.

'Fit de ye mean?' asked Jake, 'come on, spit it oot.'

'It was glowing, high up there in the crossbeams of the viaduct, like a ghost. I mean, I don't believe in all of that, but I mean I don't know…it was just floating there and moaning…' said the Stingman.

'OK,' said Jake, looking sceptical, 'but faur's the beer? Dinna tell me the ghostie wis a druth.' The Stingman was about to answer when the door of the bothy flew open causing both students, their nerves in tatters, to jump out of their seats.

*

'Aye, well Robbie,' said Gonzo, when he'd been apprised of Robbie's scheme with the black bin bag and the luminescent paint, 'you wouldn't be laughing quite so loud if you knew what that paint's doing to your health.'

'Fit's at yer saying?' asked Robbie, wiping the tears of laughter from his eyes.

'That paint's radioactive. It'll gie you cancer. It'll make your hair fall oot and yer family jewels drop off.'

'Och, yer havering min,' said Robbie dismissively.

'Have you never heard of the Radium Girls or the phossy jaw?' Robbie had not. Jake, who never really liked to see Robbie riding too high, reminded him that Gonzo had just completed the first year of a Chemistry degree at the University of Aberdeen.

Ten minutes later Robbie had disposed of the tin of luminescent paint in the large council rubbish bin beside the viaduct and, though the worry of cancer and emasculation had taken some of the gloss off his revenge, he judged that overall he'd definitely had the better of the exchange with the students, until, that was, the next evening when he was driving the Sikoda back from his most ambitious journey yet: a trip with his mother to see his maiden aunt in Inverness. Spurred on by the problem-free journey up the A96, Robbie drove his mother and aunt to see the Hydro Scheme at Foyers before returning to her home in the Culduthel part of town where his aunt cooked them all mince, tatties and peas which he ate on a tray as he watched *The Dirty Dozen* on her new 21 inch colour television.

By the time Robbie and his mother left Inverness it was getting dark, however, it wasn't until they arrived home in Bogmoor that Robbie realised why people from Nairn onwards had been tooting their horns as well as pointing and shouting at the car. When he discovered that someone had written 'The Shagging Wagon' in luminescent paint down both wings of the Sikoda Estelle.

The Unmentionables

SANDY GEDDES, the skipper of the Summer Crew, and his first mate, Robbie, were examining the Bridge Pool at the end of a long, hard day's work. It had rained heavily in the Cairngorms over the preceding two days and, though the Spey wasn't exactly in spate, it was well up, and the black water, rippling like the flank of a prize bull in the main ring at the Keith Show, swept under the railway viaduct, pinning a raft of broken branches and reeds to the upstream side of the dressed stone piers.

'It'll be gey teuch work again the morn,' said Robbie, with some relish, looking over at the rest of the Summer Crew who were lying shattered on the grass by the bothy.

'Aye, mebbe we should load up and shoot the river doon fae Fochabers the morn,' said Sandy, 'the fush'll be running herd again.'

Sandy's reasoning proved impeccable and when they got

back down to the bothy at the end of the next day the coble was loaded to the gunwales with fresh-run fish sparkling in the late-afternoon sun. As the crew were boxing the catch, a bottle-green Range Rover pulled onto the grass by the bothy and two well-heeled looking gentlemen got out. One, a tall, thin athletic man wearing a crisp new green Barbour jacket, approached Jake.

'I say…you don't happen to work on the salmon fishery do you?' asked the tall man, running a hand across his thinning pate.

'Aye, aye…' said Jake, distracted by the sight of the tall man's much shorter companion who was dressed in a remarkable outfit consisting of mustard yellow plus fours, a bright red waistcoat with silver buttons, a green tweed jacket and an oversized purple tartan Tam O'Shanter with what looked to be the majority of a pheasant's tail sticking from the head band.

'Och will ye look at that,' said Jake to Corbie, 'if it's nae the verra Cock o the North himsel.'

'Jolly good, jolly good,' said the taller man clearly not understanding a word Jake was saying, 'look, we're on the Laird's beat for the next fortnight and old Hector the ghillie said it would be a good idea to come down and talk to you chaps seeing as you might know where the fish were lying. You know, help us catch some fish.'

'Och, if it's fush yer efter, fit aboot a wee suppy Cymag,' said Jake with a mischievous glint in his eye.

'Sorry old boy, didn't quite catch that,' said the tall man uneasily, perhaps realising that Jake was being less than straight with him.

'Fit aboot yersel Corbie? Ye're the rod fisher, ye can tell

the boy fit he's needin te kaen.' Corbie scowled and said nothing, however, before Jake could say anything else, Sandy intervened.

'Hello there, I'm the skipper of the crew,' he said, edging Jake to one side, and offering the tall man his hand, 'how can I help you?'

*

As the bottle-green Range Rover pulled away up the track, Corbie spat on the ground.

'Ye wis fair sooking up te thon toffs,' he said to Sandy with some disgust, 'gnepping awa like ye wis back at the school.'

'I dinna kaen why ye dinna jist play alang wi them,' said Sandy shaking his head.

It is often assumed that fly fishing for salmon is a solely upper-class pursuit, but this is not entirely the case: local people living in the villages near the big salmon rivers of Scotland are often allowed to fish the nearby 'Town' or 'Association' waters, with permits much sought after. The salmon crews on the Spey also had the right to fish the Association water, though only a few exercised the right on account of it being too much like a busman's holiday. One of those who did was Corbie who, at least twice a week, would cycle over the Viaduct a couple of hours before a shift and fish the pools around the Bridge. In fact, Corbie spent so much time fishing the river one way or another that his knowledge of where the fish lay and how best to catch them was probably unparalleled on the lower Spey. Not that he was keen to share what he knew.

'I'd nivir tell the toffs faur the fush is lying. Thon's oor ain fush yer geen awa. Fush that local boys should hiv hid.'

'Aye, aye, it's aa verra weel fur you Corbie, but yer nae permanent, and at the end o the day, thon boys could get me ma jotters...'

'Och, that jist havers, Sandy.'

'Aa the same, it disna herm te keep in wi the rods,' replied Sandy slipping the bottle of Macallan 10 year old which had just come into his possession into the boot of his car.

Two mornings later the rod fishermen were back. The taller of the two bounded out of the car and grabbed Sandy by the hand while the Cock o the North, dressed in similarly astonishing raiment, remained in the car.

'Look Sandy, old boy, I just want to thank you,' he said effusively, 'I took five fish yesterday. Fresh-run grilse. Sea lice still on them. Everywhere else was dead as a dodo. Except Essil Pool. Exactly where you said.'

'Yes, yes, but it was you that caught them, not me,' said Sandy magnanimously.

'Well, yes of course, but all the same...'

'Not a problem. Not a problem,' said Sandy, bending down to unlock the coble. When he stood up again, he was surprised to find the tall man still hanging around.

'Is there anything else I can help you with?' asked Sandy reaching into his pocket for his pipe.

'Well actually, yes there is...the thing is that Johnny – he's the chap in the car – he's new to the game. Bought all the gear. Keen as mustard. Hasn't caught a thing. Not a sniff. Now, I think I know the problem, but that's where I need some help.'

*

'Sorry Sandy, did you just say you want a pair of women's knickers?' said Gonzo incredulously.

'Wheesht min,' said Sandy looking furtive, 'I dinna want this gettin roon.'

'You're nae some some sort of pervert are you?' asked Gonzo.

'Absolutely not,' said Sandy indignantly, 'it's fur the toffs, nae me.'

'Are they perverts?' asked the Stingman.

'No, no, no boys, it's for the oestrogen,' said Sandy.

'And why would they want that?' asked the Stingman, fearing that the skipper of the Summer Crew had lost his mind.

'Because,' said Sandy, 'aa the biggest salmon hiv bin cocht by wifeys.'

And what Sandy said was true: the record for the heaviest salmon caught by rod and line in the British Isles is held by Miss Georgina Ballantine who landed the monster 64 pound fish after a ten hour struggle on the banks of the River Tay in 1922; and the record for a salmon caught on the fly is also held by a woman – a $61^{1/2}$ pound whopper caught by Mrs Tiny Morison on the Mountblairy beat of the River Deveron in Banffshire. Indeed, several more of the largest salmon ever caught in British waters have been landed by women – a group greatly in the minority in the salmon fishing community.

No one is absolutely sure why women have been so much more successful than men when it comes to catching big salmon, however, many men have concluded – having discounted the notion that it might be down to skill on the woman's part – that the fish, as Sandy explained to the students, are attracted to the female hormone, oestrogen. Whether this is true or not is debatable, however, many game fishermen, in order to dupe the fish, keep their tackle – fishing tackle that is – in a pair of their wife's unmention-ables: one thing that was not for sale in the fancy Mayfair shop where the Cock o the North had bought his outfit.

'Couldn't you just take a pair of Meg's knickers?' said Gonzo when Sandy had finished explaining the situation. A pained look crossed Sandy's face.

'Boys, there's £10 in it for each of ye, if ye can produce a pair of wifey's unmentionables for first thing the morn's morn.'

After the shift finished, the Stingman and Gonzo retired to the pool room of the Garmouth Hotel to work out a plan of action and to spend their, as yet unearned, windfall.

'What about your aunty?' Gonzo asked the Stingman who was lodging with his aunt for the summer.

'Or your mother?' said the Stingman wincing.

'O.K, no family,' said Gonzo with a slight shudder.

'What about your lady friend from Portgordon?' asked the Stingman. Gonzo shook his head, 'she's in Magaluf for two weeks, and besides, she doesn't really wear any knickers.'

Several pints and games of pool later and suddenly clos-ing time was upon the two students and they still weren't any closer to having secured the unmentionables.

'I say we just steal a pair off a washing line,' said Gonzo as they left the pub.

'Aye, but Sandy said they had to be unwashed, you know, for the oestrogen.'

'I'll stick them in the cat's basket for the night. Nobody'll be any the wiser.'

After a short walk around the village, the Stingman and Gonzo found what they were looking for: a house with a line full of washing, including several pairs of surprisingly scant and lacy women's knickers. Unfortunately, as neither Gonzo nor the Stingman were resident in the village they didn't know whose house they were pilfering from, and they had scaled the large paling fence and reached the washing line when Rocky the Rottweiler skidded round the corner of the conservatory.

'Oh my god,' said the Stingman, taking to his heels, ploughing straight through a bed of newly planted poly-anthus and flinging himself over the tall wooden fence in the manner of an army recruit on an assault course. Gonzo wasn't so quick, and though he made it onto the fence, the dog managed to grab the heel of his wader and, feeling the jaws of the beast tighten, there was nothing Gonzo could do but straighten his foot and let the dog have his prize.

*

First thing the next morning, Sandy sidled up to Gonzo.

'Did ye get fit I wanted?'

'Aye, but there's a problem.'

'Fit's that?'

'I've lost one of my waders.'

Half an hour later, the Summer Crew were ready for the first shot of the day, but the rod fishermen still hadn't appeared. Sandy slipped the black lacy pants back to Gonzo.

'OK, you hing roon the bothy till the Super appears wi yer new widers, and if the toffs come, gie them the unmentionables and taak the money. And dinna try te swick me, or ye'll be the werse fur it.'

Sure enough, as the Summer Crew were shooting the lower Bridge Pool, the rod fishermen appeared.

'I say, you haven't seen Sandy have you?' asked the taller of the two.

'Yes, he's down there, but I think I've got what you're looking for,' replied Gonzo, reaching into his pocket and producing the lacy briefs.

'Splendid, splendid,' said the tall man shoving them into his pocket.

'Actually, they're my girlfriend's…'

'Oh, well, yeah,' said the tall man handing the £50 over to Gonzo, 'and er, thank her from us.'

Five minutes after the rod fishermen had disappeared the Super turned up with the new waders.

'Is it you needs the new widers?' he asked gruffly.

'Yes, I managed to put a hole in the other one.'

'Right, that'll be £60.'

'What?' said Gonzo.

'Ye get ae pair free wi the job; replacement pairs are £60 each. If ye've nae got it on ye, gie it te Sandy by the end o the wik, or I'll dock it fae yer pey.' And though Gonzo was tempted to give the Super the unmentionable money, he thought that it was best not to get on the wrong side of Sandy.

*

Two days later, Sandy and Robbie were patching a net holed during the recent high water when the bottle-green Range Rover pulled up outside the bothy once again.

'Sandy, Sandy there you are,' said the tall man, springing out of the car.

'What is it?' asked Sandy, a little alarmed by the man's enthusiasm.

'This is for you, and this is for the chap over there who got the knickers,' he said brandishing two £50 notes as he pointed at Gonzo.

'Aye, but ye've already paid us…'

'I know, but yesterday,' said the tall rod fisherman, putting his arm around the shoulders of the Cock o the North, who was wearing yet another remarkable outfit, 'Johnny here, landed a fifty two and a half pound salmon. It's the largest fish caught on that beat in over fifty years. One of the largest ever caught on the Spey.' The Cock o the North smiled diffidently, the pheasant feathers in his Tam O'Shanter fluttering in the light breeze.

'Nae the monster…' said Robbie turning to Sandy.

'Nivir,' said Sandy.

'It must be,' said Robbie.

'Was it blind in one eye?' asked Sandy tentatively.

'How did you know that?' said the tall rod fisherman with a look of surprise.

As the bottle-green Range Rover pulled away, Sandy, still grim-faced at the thought that the great fish had fallen to the Cock o the North, turned to Gonzo, 'I dinna kaen fit you're grinning aboot,' he said, 'I'll hae that £50 fur the widers. And ye still owe me a tenner.'

The Rave at Rothes

WHEN SANDY GEDDES, the skipper of the Summer Crew, arrived for the early shift he found the bothy in uproar. Corbie was swearing and cursing with even greater vigour than was usual, and for once even the Neap seemed animated.

'Fit on earth is gan on here?' asked Sandy, standing in the doorway of the bothy, surveying the commotion.

'MoJo's gan te Rangers,' said Jake holding up the front page of his newspaper which related the news that the former Celtic football player Maurice 'MoJo' Johnston had, after spells at both Watford and Nantes, decided to sign for Rangers rather than re-sign for his former team, Celtic, as he had suggested he would, thereby making him one of only a handful of Catholics to sign for Rangers since the 1920s.

'It's a total disgrace,' cried Corbie, a Rangers fan, 'he's a

Catholic.'

'He's a Judas,' said the Neap, a Celtic fan, 'he's nithing but a Judas.'

As the two salmon fishers expressed their indignation at the signing, Robbie leant over to Gonzo.

'Could ye jist sign this bitty paper, please,' said Robbie, offering him a well-chewed bookie's pen and a grubby old airmail envelope.

'Sorry,' said Gonzo, looking at Robbie, 'why do want my signature?'

'Och, nae reason, I jist like te collect the signatures o abdy fa works on the salmon fishing,' replied Robbie. Gonzo looked sceptical.

'He should be banned fae Scottish football,' said the Neap.

'Come on, jist sign it,' said Robbie, thrusting the envelope at Gonzo.

'Then he should be castrated and hung up on Glesga Green,' said Corbie.

'I kaen why he's needin yer signature,' said Jake to Gonzo, 'he's needin te kaen fa painted "Shagging Wagon" on the wings o his car in thon fluorescent paint. He wants te compare the handwriting.'

'That's nae true,' said Robbie vehemently, 'I jist want te get a record o aa the boys' signatures. You kaen hoo I appreciate guid handwriting.'

'You don't think it was me that wrote on your car, do you?' asked Gonzo, seemingly genuinely surprised by the implication.

'Aye, if ye mist kaen, I do, I mean, fa else wid dee it?'

'Castration is too good for the likes o him,' said the Neap.

'Yer nae wrang, he should be castrated, shot and then

hung up on Glesga Green,' said Corbie.

'I was under the impression that you did it yourself,' said Gonzo to Robbie.

'Fit,' said Robbie incredulously, 'why on earth would I paint that on ma ain car?'

'Well, you're over forty and you're nae married; I thought you did it because you want to attract a mate…'

'I'm nae married because I nivir met the richt quine,' replied Robbie indignantly, 'and onywey, if I wis needin te find a wumen the last thing I'd dee is write thon nonsense doon the side o ma car.'

'That's it, I've hid enough,' said Corbie jumping to his feet and pushing his way past Robbie and out of the bothy where he produced a cigarette lighter from his pocket and proceeded to set fire to the Rangers scarf he often wore on the night shift. As the flames took hold of the cheap synthetic material the Neap joined in, setting light to a picture of MoJo he'd ripped from Jake's paper; the supporters of the two deadly footballing rivals united as never before in the face of a common enemy. Sandy, however, was deeply unsettled by the potentially divisive cocktail of sectarian and personal politics swirling round the bothy and decided that the only way to dampen the inflamed tempers of the Summer Crew was to tire them out, so, despite the fact that he hadn't had his usual morning brew or buttery roll, he took them straight out on the first of what proved to be a record number of shots in a day. By the lunch break, after taking them all the way down to the mouth and making them haul back up again twice, they were worn out, apart, that is, from Robbie, who, after a quick rummage in the council bin up by the viaduct, retrieved the pot of fluorescent paint.

'Och no Robbie, ye've nae been raking aboot in that bin hiv ye? Thon fluorescent paint his created oer muckle trouble aridy,' said Sandy, shaking his head in despair.

'No dinna worry Sandy, I'm nae up te mischief, it's jist that the gloss disna taak oer the fluorescent paint, and there's nae wey I can afford a respray.'

'So fit are ye deein?'

'I'm jist gan oer the writing wi mair fluorescent paint, te maak a big stripe, kaen. It'll be better than haeing that written on the car. I mean, I canna go onywhere at nicht since the students wrote "The Shagging Wagon" on the side o it. Fowk jist toot their horns and yell oot. And ma mither wis black affronted fan she foond oot fit it meant...'

'Will folk nae think yer the jam sandwich if ye de that?' asked Jake.

'Do the police drive Sikodas?' asked Gonzo who had been lingering in earshot. The usually sanguine Sandy hit the roof.

'Richt that's it. If there's ony mair of this nonsense wi Sikodas, Maurice Johnston or fluorescent paint, then you'll leave me nae option but to gan te the Super.' Even Robbie, who had worked with Sandy for some twenty five years had never seen him so angry, and that afternoon Gonzo and the Stingman were made to clean the coble, redd up the netbox and load the fish as well as shooting it back down to the mouth and hauling up again with the rest of the crew.

*

A couple of days later Sandy's harsh regime combined with a particularly strong grilse run had not only quieted the general disposition of the Summer Crew, but had also seen them start to catch up with the total number of fish caught by the permanent crew.

The strong grilse run continued and, seeing an opportunity to make further inroads into Brian's lead, Sandy managed to get the Super to agree to another Saturday shift. However, the younger members of the Summer Crew, shattered from their exertions and looking forward to their weekend, were none too pleased when Sandy informed them of the extra day's work. The Neap, in particular, was unimpressed as he had arranged to go up to Rothes that Friday night.

'Come on Robbie, I nivir hid onything te dee with the writin on yer car,' pleaded the Neap. Robbie looked unconvinced.

'Come on Robbie, ye telt us ye wid, I'm only needin a lift up te Rothes.'

'That wis afore ma Skoda wis vandalised.'

'That wisna me...'

'Fit are ye deein in Rothes onywey?'

'There's a rave up there the nicht.'

'A rowp?'

'No, nae a rowp, a rave.'

'And fit's that then?' asked Robbie.

'It's like a dance in a field, wi electronic techno music,' explained the Neap.

'Duncing in a park?' said Jake who had been listening in to the conversation, 'in my day we used to gan te the dunces at the hotel up at the Craig. Ye'd drink a hauf bottle ootside and if ye didna get a trap, ye'd be guaranteed a fecht. I hid some cracking fechts up there...' said Jake with a nostalgic glint in his eye.

'Naebody fechts at the raves, abdy's on ecstasy…' said the Neap.

'Dis that nae send you loop the loop?' asked Jake who had recently read an alarmist article in the paper on the nascent rave scene in the paper.

The Neap shrugged and popped another Refresher in his mouth. 'Nae really, it's nae as bad as the drink. Alcohol wid be made illegal if they tried te introduce it these days.'

'Rave music's rubbish,' said Gonzo emphatically.

'Fit's rubbish is heavy metal; it's deid. Yer living in the past.'

'Metal'll never die,' said Gonzo, emphatically.

'It could be fun though,' suggested the Stingman, 'it is a party.'

'I'm nae taakin thon twa in the car, if that's fit yer thinking,' said Robbie sharply, looking at the students.

'Oh, come oan Robbie, time te bury the hatchet. And besides, they'll pey ye on tap o fit I gie ye,' said the Neap.

*

The light was fading when Robbie dropped the three younger members of the Summer Crew in a field just outside Rothes.

'Mind, I'll be back at 5.30 am sharp, so we get doon te the fishing for the start at six…' said Robbie.

'Aye, that's fine,' said the Neap, looking round the field where a crowd of about three hundred people were gathered round a large sound system and light show.

'If yer nae here I'll jist turn roon and leave; and Sandy said if ye dinna pit in a shift the morn, ye'll aa get yer jotters.'

Having reassured Robbie, the Neap disappeared into the crowd, while Gonzo and the Stingman wandered around to check out what was going on. Gonzo was not impressed.

'Look at them, they look like idiots,' he said, referring to three young men, stripped to the waist, wearing welding googles and waving Glo Sticks in the air in front of a speaker stack pumping hardcore Dutch Gabber into the Morayshire evening air at 180 bpm.

'There's some good looking women,' observed the Stingman.

'Aye, but they're only interested in dancing,' replied Gonzo as the Neap reappeared with one of the organisers of the rave – a young Glaswegian man with neon pink hair.

'Awright man, whit ye needin, man?' he asked, looking around furtively.

*

Robbie's arrival at Rothes, at a quarter past five, caused some consternation among the rave goers, who at first thought, much as Jake had suggested might happen, that the Skoda was a police car. However, once they'd been reassured by the Neap, several of them gathered round the car.

'See that car, that's absolutely magic,' said the pink-haired rave organiser, 'it's magic, man. Look how it's glowing. It's pure, deid brilliant.'

'Aye weel, the less said aboot that the better,' said Robbie glaring at the Stingman.

'No man, I love it man, it's beautiful. It's like the most beautiful car I've ever seen, man.'

'Aye, it is good, like,' agreed Robbie, standing back and admiring his recent purchase.

'How much dae ye want fur it, man?' said the pink-haired Glaswegian who was jigging up and down to the beat of the music.

'No, I'm nae selling,' said Robbie instinctively.

'Look, I'll gie ye 500 notes, right now, man,' said the rave organiser, pulling a large roll of bills from his pocket.

'Well, ah'm nae sure…' said Robbie who had paid only £300 for the car just two weeks before.

'Right, £600.'

'Aye, but hoo are we g'te get doon te the fishing?'

'£700, that's ma final offer.'

'He'll take it,' said the Stingman hastily, shaking the rave organiser's hand.

While Robbie counted the money, the Stingman searched for Gonzo who he eventually found, stripped to the waist, dancing in front of one of the speaker stacks, wearing a pair of welding goggles and waving a Glo-stick in the air.

'The Neap was right,' shouted Gonzo, 'this is the best music in the world.'

*

That morning the younger members of the Summer Crew were somewhat more subdued than was normal. Robbie, on the other hand, was not.

'I kaent fae the moment I saw it that the Sikoda was a guid investment,' said Robbie looking very pleased with himself.

'I got £700 for the car, that's £400 mair than I paid fur it…and I bargained him richt up, did I?' he said turning to the Stingman.

'You played him like a fiddle,' muttered the Stingman,

who just wanted to catch twenty minutes sleep in between shots.

'That's right, he wanted to gie me £500, but I bargained him up te £700. And aa I hid te dee wis pey fur a taxi doon here.'

'It mist hiv been like watching the great fiddler Willie McPherson himsel,' said Jake winking at the students.

*

The next weekend, Gonzo made the trip into Elgin and bought half a dozen 12 inch rave tracks, however, halfway through listening to the second one he realised that his damascene conversion in a field near Rothes might have been a little hasty. As he was heard to comment later, 'rave music's total rubbish unless you're aff yer heid.'

Just over a week after the rave at Rothes, the pink-haired organiser was stopped on the M8 where the police, upon searching the Skoda, found a bag containing 50 Ecstasy tablets. He was charged with 'possession with intent to supply' and the Skoda was confiscated under the proceeds of crime provisions in the Criminal Justice Act 1988. A couple of months later, in his second Old Firm game Maurice Johnston scored a decisive goal for his new team and sealed his place in the Rangers fans' affections, causing the notoriously parsimonious Corbie to sorely regret his decision to burn his scarf and the Neap to demand that all mention of Johnson be expunged from the Celtic record books. At the end of the summer, just before he went back to university, Gonzo sold his six rave 12 inches to the Neap for a third of their face value.

The Affair of the Spent Hens

SANDY GEDDES, the skipper of the Summer Crew, pulled the collar of his donkey jacket up around his ears and stepped out of the bothy door into the bitter, blustery wind. To the north, over the leaden sea, towering cumulonimbus storm clouds, known thereabouts as the Banff bailiffs, as they kept the deep-sea boats in port and their crews' pockets empty, piled up on the horizon. Sandy shuddered in the cold and retreated back into the bothy.

'Fit's it look like?' asked Jake.

'We'll dee ae mair shot in aboot twenty minutes and then cry it a day,' said Sandy stepping over to the pot-bellied stove which stood in the middle of the bothy, 'it looks like it's g'te be gey roch later on.'

As Sandy warmed the backs of his legs against the stove, the talk in the bothy turned to money; more specifically, the money Robbie had made selling his Skoda the week before.

'Sandy, fit wid ye dee wi the £300 Robbie jist made?' asked Corbie.

'I'd pit it in the bank,' said Sandy who was by nature risk averse.

'Fit aboot Premium Bonds?' asked the Neap.

'Premium Bonds,' snorted Corbie, 'ye'd jist spend it on Caramel Logs,' he continued uncharitably.

'You could throw a big party,' said Gonzo. Robbie shook his head.

'I'm nae ge te de ony o thon things, I'm thinking o buying a Mark II Escort.'

'Och, ye canna get a daecent een fur fit ye've got,' said Corbie, 'ye'd need anither £300 on tap fur at.' Robbie nodded his assent.

'Aye, yer nae wrang,' he said, looking thoughtful.

'You're so fill o it, Corbie; fit wid ye dee?' asked Jake.

'I'd invest it,' said Corbie sagely.

'Fit in?'

'Spent hens.'

'Spent hens...' said Robbie quizzically, 'fit are they?'

'Battery hen's fit's deen wi laying, I can get them in bulk fur twenty pince a bird and sell em fur a poon.'

'That sounds a wee bitty chancey te me,' said Robbie sceptically.

'Mebbe, but sometimes ye've got te speculate te accumulate,' said Corbie.

'Aye weel, if there's ae thing that's sure, it's that a man wi money nivir lacks fur advice aboot fit te dee wi it,' said Sandy as he turned around to face the stove and warm his hands.

'Fit aboot you Stingman. Fit wid ye dee?' asked Corbie.

'Sorry, what was that?' said the Stingman who was sitting on the nets in the corner of the bothy trying to make some early inroads into the coming year's course reading list.

'Fit wid ye spend Robbie's three hunner on?'

'I'd pay off my overdraft,' said the Stingman looking back down at his book.

'Fit's that yer reading?' asked Corbie.

The Stingman held up his copy of *The Canterbury Tales* to show him the cover.

'Fit's *The Canterbury Tales* fan it's at hame?' asked Corbie, squinting as he read the title. The Stingman sighed.

'It's a set of stories told by a group of pilgrims on their way from London to Canterbury Cathedral in the 14th century.'

'Is that fit they teach ye at the University?' asked Corbie. The Stingman nodded.

'So, let me get this straight, you're English, but ye've come up te a Scottish university te study English. That's Irish, if you ask me.'

'Och, wheesht wull ye Colin,' said Sandy coming to the Stingman's defence, 'he bides in England, but he wis born up here and his femily hiv bid up here as far back as yours or mine. He's a Moray loon.'

'And even if I am English what difference does that make?' said the Stingman, angered by the steady drip of anti-English sentiment he'd had to endure since he moved north of the border, 'if you judge me by where I come from, instead of who I am, then you're a racist.'

'Aye weel, I still dinna see fit the point is o studying nuvels and poems,' said Corbie unhappily. The Stingman shook his head but said nothing; even though he wasn't entirely sure what the point of studying literature was himself, it wasn't something he was about to debate with Corbie.

'Are ye g'te read us a wee bitty then?' asked Jake. The Stingman shook his head.

'No, I couldn't.' The rest of the crew rallied behind Jake.

'Come on Stingman, gie's a couple o lines.'

The Stingman looked dubious, but turned back to the beginning of the poem.

'O.K, this one's the Reeve's Tale.'

'Fit's a Reeve?' asked Robbie.

'It's like an estate manager.'

'Like the Super?'

'Maybe more like his boss, the Factor,' said the Stingman as he looked back down at his book before clearing his throat and launching into his best Middle English.

> 'At Trumpyngtoun, nat fer fro Cantebrigge,
> Ther gooth a brook, and oer that a brigge,
> Upon the whiche brook ther stant a melle;
> And this is verray sooth that I yow telle.'

'That's the wey they speak oer in Turra,' said Robbie, looking astonished, 'I swear te God, it's like my cousin fae Auchterless is in the room wi us the noo.' Sandy held his finger up to his lips and looked at Robbie, then back at the Stingman.

'Oh, aye sorry, go on,' said Robbie apologetically. The Stingman started again.

> 'A millere was ther dwellynge many a day.
> As any pecok he was proud and gay.

> Pipen he koude and fisshe, and nettes beete
> And turne coppes, and wel wrastle and sheete;'

'Noo, I didna quite get that bit...' said Robbie shaking his head, 'but then I dinna really understaun ma cousin fae Auchterless hauf the time.'

'It says that the miller could play the bagpipes and fish and mend nets...he liked a drink, and he could wrestle and shoot.'

'That's the kind o boy we need in the Summer Crew,' said Jake, 'he plays the pipes, Corbie, even though he's English.' Corbie looked unimpressed.

'I dinna understand fit the point o studying nuvels is,' he said again, causing the Stingman to point out that irrespective of whether Corbie saw the point or not, he was funding the Stingman's grant, and therefore study of literature, with the taxes he paid. A revelation which caused much consternation among the Summer Crew who were only calmed when Sandy forced them out into the biting north-easterly for the final shot of the day.

*

The next day Robbie and Corbie walked into the bothy with broad smiles on their faces.

'Fit are you pair looking sae smug aboot?' asked the Neap.

'Me and Corbie,' said Robbie, 'we've jist bocht fifteen hunner spent hens.'

'Really...' said Sandy sceptically, 'fit are ye g'te dee wi them?'

'We're keeping them on Jake's ferm, til we sell em.'

'Is that richt?' asked Sandy, turning to Jake.

'Aye,' said Jake, 'they're rentin een o ma byres.'

'And fan I've selt them, I'll easy hae enough for a daecent Mark II Escort,' said Robbie cheerfully.

However, Robbie was not quite so enthusiastic when the hens were delivered two days later. Old battery hens are a pitiful sight: featherless, debeaked and distressed, many have broken bones and few can stand properly. The bottom of the trailer was littered with birds which had died on the short journey from the battery farm just outside Elgin.

'Are you sure this is aa richt?' asked Robbie, who was at heart an animal lover and quite upset by the sight of the suffering birds.

'Aye, dinna fash yersel,' said Corbie, kicking one of the dead birds off the trailer, 'I factored in fur a puckley deid eens.'

For the next three days Robbie cycled up to Jake's farm every morning to feed the birds. It troubled him every time he saw them huddled in the corner of the barn, and he began to wish that he'd taken Sandy, the Neap's, or even Gonzo's investment advice. Robbie's dark mood was deepened when the advert went in *The Northern Scot* that Friday, as by the Saturday evening they had sold a mere ten birds.

'I canna believe I listened te Corbie,' said Robbie to himself, as he tried to work out how much he might lose if the birds kept selling at the same rate.

The next day, as the Summer Crew stood round the net-box getting ready for the first shot of the day, Robbie and Corbie tried to persuade Jake to lower the rent on the barn. Jake refused.

'Sorry boys, but business is business, yer aridy getting a highly preferential rate.'

'I dinna kaen fit we're g'te dee,' moaned Corbie, who had also invested some money from his Post Office savings account in the venture, 'we could lose aathin.'

'I might be able to help you,' said the Stingman.

'Fit wey?' asked Corbie suspiciously.

'Corbie, calm doon, listen te the boy, he's trying te help ye…' said Jake.

'So fit is it ye think ye can dee?' asked Robbie.

'Well, look at your advert for a start,' said the Stingman, 'what does it say?'

'Spent hens. Call Robbie. Bogmoor 284.' The Stingman shook his head.

'So fit's awrang wi that?' asked Corbie defensively.

'Well, "spent hens", for a start that's not an appealing concept. You'll sell nothing if you keep on calling them that.'

'So fit wid you say?' The Stingman thought for a moment.

'Prime roasters…casserole chickens… maybe something like that, and the name, I would change the "Call Robbie" bit as well, to something like Call Speymouth Quality Foods. It sounds more professional. And get rid of Bogmoor too, it doesn't sound like somewhere you'd get quality food from, put in the area code instead.' Corbie looked sceptical. 'That's oer lang, we pey by the character fur thon advert, that's g'te cost us a fortune.'

'Maybe Corbie, but sometimes you've got to speculate to accumulate,' replied the Stingman.

*

That Saturday the phone never stopped ringing, with 'Prime Roasters' and 'Casserole Chickens' literally flying out of the door. The next Monday, Robbie and Corbie were delighted.

'Aye weel,' conceded Corbie, 'mebbe there is some yees in studying nuvels.' The Stingman felt more equivocal about the use of his literary talents for the sale of spent hens, however, he was pleased to get Corbie off his back.

Robbie and Corbie were less pleased when, four weeks later, they discovered that the poor start and a higher than expected mortality rate had diminished their profits by such a degree that both men lost over £100 each on the enterprise. Which, coupled with a higher than expected Poll Tax bill, lead Robbie to conclude that a new car would be too great an expense for the moment, and that he would be better off with a motorbike again.

The only member of the Summer Crew who was truly happy with the affair of the spent hens was Jake who had rented Robbie and Corbie his barn.

The Maggie Fair

THE MAGGIE FAIR is held in the village of Garmouth every summer. It's the big social event of the year in the local area, and the streets in the centre of the village are lined with an assortment of produce and bric-a-brac stalls, and the park at the bottom of the brae is home to the games, displays and beer tent.

At half past one the host of the breakfast show on Moray Firth Radio, Donny 'Mad Dog' MacDonald, after delivering a short speech reminding everyone of the four hundred year history of the Maggie Fair and that they could catch him and his 'Madhouse Posse' weekdays from 6 am til 9 am on 96.6 on FM or 1107 on the MW band, rang the Maggie Fair bell to indicate the opening of the stalls. As soon as the bell rang, the Neap who, along with the Stingman and Gonzo, had taken up position at the front of the bottle stall, bought £5 worth of tickets with the intention of winning a bottle of whisky. Three minutes later, having discovered that he hadn't won, the Neap rummaged in his wallet and pulled out a second £5 note.

'Come on, you'd be as well going to the shop to buy it,' said the Stingman, but the Neap wouldn't be dissuaded and when he discovered that the whisky had eluded him for a second time, he pulled his wallet out again. This time, however, the Stingman and Gonzo intervened.

'No, we've got the Tug o' War at two fifteen,' said Gonzo.

'Jist ae mair shotty,' said the Neap as Gonzo and the Stingman pulled him away.

*

Acting as compere for the games in the park was Alan Thain, the flamboyant manager of a hotel in Fochabers where he hosted a fortnightly 'Scottish Historical Pageant' during which he changed costume with each of the dozen courses and regaled guests with jokes and songs, culminating in the highlight of the evening – a karaoke rendition of *Charlie is my Darling* featuring *mein host* dressed, resplendent in full tartan regalia, as the fugitive Jacobite prince.

Outside the beer tent the older members of the Summer Crew – Sandy, Robbie, Corbie and Jake – were discussing the likely outcome of the under-fifteen boys' sack race, as Alan Thain, dressed in a powder-blue mohair suit, set off nicely by a pair of monogrammed, lemon-yellow slip-on shoes, introduced the contestants.

'I reckon Wullie Flett's loon'll win,' said Robbie, casting his eye over the entrants, lined up holding the sacks around their waists.

'Aye, Thain's got him as odds-on favourite,' said Corbie,

'though sack racing can be gey chancey, ae fa and it's aa oer.' As Corbie expounded further on the finer points of sack racing, Robbie spotted the three younger members of the Summer Crew queuing at the bar in the beer tent.

'Hey, fit de ye think yer deeing?' he shouted, striding over to where they stood.

'We're haeing a beer,' said Gonzo.

'Oh no yer nae,' said Robbie, 'nae afore the Tug o' War.'

'Corbie's drinking,' observed the Neap.

'That's as mebbe, but you loons are nae drinking a drap til the Tug o' War is deen, and that's that. The pride of the Summer Crew is at stake.'

So, lemonades in hand, the Neap, the Stingman and Gonzo joined the older members of the Summer Crew as they watched the finish of the under-fifteens' sack race in which, to Alan Thain's evident disappointment, Wullie Flett's son literally ran away with it.

'Look at Thainy, he's nae haeing a guid day, aa the favourites is comin in. He'll be rooked the night,' said Corbie revelling in the bookmaker's misfortune.

'So did ye win the bottle o whisky?' asked Sandy. The Neap shook his head.

'Did ye win onything?'

'Aye,' said the Neap staring despondently at the carrier bag by his feet, 'I won a bottle o Hay's Ice Cream Soda, twa jars o Baxter's crinkle cut pickled beetroot, een oot o date jar of reed currant jeely and a pot o Vasoline. I coulda bocht it aa in the shops fur less than hauf the price.'

'Weel, look on the bright side, Neil, ye can aye use the vaseline wi a quiney if ye can iver find een,' said Jake.

'Ha, ha...verra funny,' said the Neap, opening a jar of

pickled beetroot and scooping a couple of slices into his mouth with his fingers, as Brian, the temporary skipper of the permanent crew, appeared round the side of the beer tent.

'Boys, there ye are,' said Brian, 'I jist came te wush ye luck.'

'That's awfa kind o ye Brian, but it's you lot that'll be needin' it,' said Robbie. Brian laughed, 'aye Robbie, it'd be a different story if ye werna banned fae the competition, but thon three young loons couldna lift a fushbox a few wiks ago.'

What Brian said was true, with Robbie on the team the Summer Crew would have easily wiped the floor with all-comers; not only was he six foot nine and seventeen stone of lean muscle, he had, as a younger man, competed on the Highland Games circuit with some considerable success. Unfortunately, Robbie had been banned from competing at the Maggie Fair as the consequence of a very unfortunate incident during the haggis-hurling competition some five years before. It was, everyone agreed, a freak accident – no one had any idea that someone could hurl a haggis that far, and even though it had hit the man on the side of the head, things might still have been OK if the haggis hadn't been sitting in the freezer of a certain hotelier only half an hour before, or if Donny 'Mad Dog' MacDonald hadn't broadcast the incident live to his not insubstantial listener base around the Moray Firth.

In the furore that ensued, Robbie was banned for life from the Maggie Fair games by the organising committee, even though, after a short enquiry, the police exonerated him from any culpability for the man's injuries. In addition, the incident provided a rich seam of humour for the 'Madhouse Posse' who mined it mercilessly for several weeks until their attention was diverted by news of a farmer from South Ronaldsay who had found a turnip that looked like the then Chancellor of the Exchequer, Nigel Lawson.

Robbie was furious for months that in the eyes of the public, if not the law, he was the person to whom blame was apportioned: as he put it himself whenever the subject was raised, 'I wis hung oot te dry.'

*

As the two salmon fishing crews lined up for the first semi-final of the Tug o' War – there being only four teams in the whole competition and the two fishing crews having drawn one another – Brian taunted Sandy, 'nae only are we echt boxes aheid o ye on the fishing, we're ge te baet ye hollow in the Tug o' War. It'll be a clean sweep fur the permanent crew this year.'

'Aye, time will tell Brian, time will tell,' said Sandy taking a sip of beer.

'Fit chance hiv we got?' asked Sandy as Brian walked off to give some last minute encouragement to the permanent crew.

'Slim te none, and slim's oot o toon,' said Corbie shaking his head pessimistically.

Robbie shrugged, 'I widna say that, Jake's wee, bit he's een o the strangest cheils I iver rowed wi, and the young loons is a lot stranger than fan they jined the fushing, and fae fit I've seen since I've been coaching them in the last couple o wiks, I'd say it micht be werth laying a wee bet wi Mr Thain oer there.'

It wasn't long, however, before Sandy began to regret listening to Robbie's advice, as the first pull of the three was over almost before it started when Gonzo let go of the rope causing the Summer Crew to be routed.

'Fit wey did ye let go, Gonzo?' asked Robbie angrily, as the permanent crew celebrated their win.

'It was the Neap, he burped, and the smell of the beetroot put me off.'

'It wis the ice cream soda repeating on me,' explained the Neap.

Sandy reached into his pocket, 'aye weel Neil, here's a couple of Pandrops, get sooking,' he said as Robbie gathered the Summer Crew round and outlined his preferred strategy for the second pull.

The second pull was a different story, not only did the Pandrops settle the Neap's stomach, but the Summer Crew, following Robbie's instructions, dug in and held their position while the permanent crew, brimming with confidence, tried to pull themselves to what they thought would be a second easy victory and a place in the final. When, after about five minutes of deadlock, Robbie judged that the permanent crew had blown themselves out, he called to the Summer Crew.

'Richt boys, let's haal the fushes in,' he shouted, then watched as slowly, inexorably, and to the astonishment of the crowd, the Summer Crew pulled a tiring permanent crew over the line. The third pull was a formality. The permanent crew, still exhausted from their efforts in the second pull, offered little resistance and when Sandy looked round there was no sign of Brian, who had suddenly remembered that he had to help his wife up on the cake stall.

As Corbie picked up his and Sandy's winnings, Alan

Thain lamented his own bad fortune.

'That is the only upset of the entire day. Every other favourite's won. I'm going to lose a fortune; this has been a bad day for me Corbie, a very bad day.'

The second semi-final was a foregone conclusion, with the farmers thrashing the team from the Royal Oak in Urquhart in two straight pulls, and further compounding Alan Thain's misery.

*

The final of the Tug o' War was the highlight of the games. Despite the Summer Crew's sensational earlier victory, they had no backers among the beer tent pundits who had all backed the farmers, the lightest of whom was Dode Mann, weighing in at sixteen stone ten in his stocking soles.

'Och boys, jist enjoy yersels, ye've baet the permanent crew and that's fit coonts,' said Robbie as the Summer Crew took to the field. As Corbie walked past, Sandy stopped him.

'Hey Corbie, faur's ma money?' he asked.

'Och, I decided to let it ride on the Summer Crew for the final.'

'Fit?' said Sandy incredulously.

'Thainy's offering 10-1 against the Summer Crew. We could win a fortune,' said Corbie calmly.

'Och Corbie, ye've got a touch o the sun or something. There's nae wey we can baet the fermers, look at the size o them. Yer supposed to be the grippet een, nae the een fa throws guid money doon the drain.'

'Dinna be sae pessimistic,' said Corbie in a surprisingly sanguine fashion as he walked off to take his place at the front of the rope.

As they lined up, a very relaxed looking Summer Crew accepted the plaudits of the crowd who had all got behind the clear underdog. However, soon after both teams took the strain, the crowd was surprised to find the farmers quickly losing ground and before they knew it the Summer Crew had won the first pull. The farmers were in uproar.

'We can't get a hud o the rope, there's something nae richt,' complained Dode Mann. Alan Thain looked at the rope.

'It seems alright to me,' he said.

'No it's nae, it's nae richt, look, it's aa slippy...'

'Look, come on boys, I've heard all the excuses in the book. If you don't take your place for the second pull within the allotted two minutes, you'll forfeit the final,' said Alan Thain as he adjusted his diamante tie pin and coolly ran his hand through his carefully coiffured mane of thick, black hair.

*

The celebrations went on late into the night, and such were the high spirits that even Corbie bought a round with the winnings from the bet that Alan Thain was only too happy to pay out, it being a tenth the size of the payout he had been liable for if the farmers had won. In fact, such a good time was had by all of the crew, that when the Neap got home to Tugnet much later on that night, he didn't even realise that the jar of Vaseline was missing from his bag of winnings from the bottle stall.

The Obscenity

ONE FINE SATURDAY morning, Mr R M Mackintosh (B Eng), the Assistant Director of Roads for Moray Council, and three-time club captain of the Garmouth and Kingston Golf Club, was walking his black Labrador, Sweep, on the old railway embankment leading to the viaduct and trying to recall whether the swallows flying low over the field below forecast good or bad weather, when he saw it, trampled in the barley in letters 30 feet high.

'It's an obscenity,' he said, tucking his paper under his arm as he stood in the Post Office a little later, 'I've spoken to George, whose field it is, and he assures me that he will get to it as soon as he can, but, in the meantime, I would strongly recommend that you avoid the area when you take Moss out for his walk.'

'Just out of curiosity, can you tell me what it says?' asked

Miss Sylvia Main, Garmouth's newsagent and postmistress.

'Oh, no, no, it's a word that no woman should ever have to hear,' said Mr R M Mackintosh, adding as he turned to leave the shop, 'oh yes, and you'd be doing the village a great favour if you were to pass this information on to your other customers by way of a warning.' As if there was the remotest chance that Miss Main would keep such a piece of information to herself.

After his tea that night, Mr R M Mackintosh tried to call George the farmer to determine what progress had been made on erasing the obscenity, however, as George didn't answer the phone, he decided to walk down and check for himself. As he descended the steps down to the railway line, he was surprised by the large number of villagers taking the air and the sight of a small crowd gathered on the embankment overlooking the obscenity.

'It's awful big letters, is it?' said Mrs Fergusson, the district nurse.

'Yes, they must have spent a fair time at that,' mused Miss Syliva Main.

'Dis onybidy kaen fa it wis?' asked Ernie Robertson, the local mechanic.

'Miss Main,' said Mr R M Mackintosh, who had joined the back of the small group, 'I'm surprised to see you over here.'

'Moss is a very wilful dog,' she said hastily, and not entirely untruthfully, 'he has a mind of his own. And he always likes his walk down by the river.'

'I see,' said Mr R M Mackintosh looking down disapprovingly at the chocolate-coloured Springer Spaniel which had jumped up on his leg.

The obscenity was still there two days later, and though local interest had long since waned, its continued presence rankled with Mr R M Mackintosh to such a degree that he raised the subject at the fortnightly meeting of the Amenities Committee that evening.

'Surely we've got mair important things to worry about,' said David 'Scoop' Shand, *Northern Scot* journalist and secretary of the committee.

'What about the tourists?' said Mr R M Mackintosh

'Tourists? No one ever comes here,' replied 'Scoop' Shand.

'There's the visiting rod fishermen, and there's folk from as far away as Keith come for the golf.'

'Well, I'm sure it's a word that the gowfers and the fishers...and even the "fowk fae Keith" have heard afore,' said 'Scoop' Shand, smiling at the other members of the committee.

'That's not the point, it's a stain on the good name of the village,' said Mr R M Mackintosh, removing his reading spectacles and rubbing his eyes.

'Well, I have to say, I agree with Mr Mackintosh,' said Jenny Felgate, wife of the vet and stalwart of many village committees, 'I went for a walk over the viaduct this morning and the obscenity was still clearly evident in the field.'

'Yes, I spoke to George again yesterday, to see if he couldn't do something about it,' said Mr R M Mackintosh, replacing his glasses, 'but he told me that he has a cow with a very bad case of mastitis and that he has better things to do than go around trampling down his own crops...I'm afraid to say that he was a little brusque.'

'I suppose that's understandable,' said Mrs Felgate wincing, 'I know how unpleasant mastitis can be.'

'Can we nae jist leave it, surely the hairst is due in a few weeks,' interjected 'Scoop' Shand, 'after all, there are other issues in the village that surely merit more of our attention...'

'No, in my opinion, it's not acceptable; first there's the bowls tournament in a couple of weeks and then the four-day Golf Open...' replied Mr R M Mackintosh.

'Does anyone know who was responsible?' asked Jenny Felgate going off at a slight tangent.

'Well, I know for a fact that the salmon fishers were on a spree in the hotel that evening, because they set fire to the Rattray's bin and rolled it down the brae,' reported 'Scoop' Shand.

'It's the Summer Crew,' said Mr R M Mackintosh nodding sagely, 'there's not a year goes by without some trouble with the Summer Crew.'

'And there was the incident with that nice young RAF couple next door to me, where they found a fisherman's wader in their garden and underwear missing from their washing line,' added Mrs Felgate.

'It seems that they're worse than usual this year,' said Mr R M Mackintosh, 'it may well get out of hand if it's not nipped in the bud.'

*

'Richt boys, I'll gie it te ye straight, there's an awfa fuss aboot something written in the crops oer by Germouth,' said Sandy, who had been on the receiving end of a lecture from the Super, who'd been interrupted in turn by a phone call from Mr R M Mackintosh just after he'd settled down to watch *True Grit* on the television the night before.

'Fit dis it say?' asked Jake.

'Weel, ye'll nivir hear me use the word, but if you listen te Corbie for a coupla minutes, you'll definitely hear it mair than aince.'

'OK, but fit's aa this got te dee wi us?' asked Jake.

'Weel, mebbe it's got nothing te dee wi you,' said Sandy pointedly as he looked round the bothy, 'but perhaps there's ither members o this crew fa kaen a lot mair aboot it.'

'Div ony o ye young loons kaen fa wrote that sweary word in the fermer's park?' asked Jake, winking at the Stingman and Gonzo.

'Maybe it wis aliens,' suggested Gonzo helpfully.

'Och, that's rubbish,' said Robbie.

'It could be,' replied Gonzo.

'Hoo's that?' asked Robbie.

'It's like the crop circles, a lot of fowk believe they're made by aliens, why nae this?'

'Fit alien is going to come down to Germouth jist te write a sweary word in some crops?' said Robbie shaking his head.

'Maybe he didn't like Garmouth.'

'Germouth's a fine place,' said Robbie.

'I never said it wisna, I just said it maybe wasn't the alien's cup of tea. Maybe he thought Kingston was better. Or Tugnet.'

'OK, OK,' said Sandy calling a halt to the debate, 'I'm no interested if it wis aliens or no, aa I'm saying is that there's pressure on the fishing at the moment because o the low salmon numbers, and the last thing onybidy needs is fowk draggin the good name o the fishers through the mud. So the word fae the Super is nae mair high jinks in the village. Noo, hiv ye aa got that clear?'

*

That night saw the arrival of the bad weather presaged by the swallows Mr R M Mackintosh had spotted flying low a couple of days before, and it was still raining the next morning, albeit lightly, when Miss Sylvia Main took Moss on his usual walk down to the river. As they followed the path through the reeds under the viaduct, Moss bounded on ahead. Halfway to the river Miss Main found her passage blocked by a small but fast-flowing channel which had risen dramatically overnight. There was no sign of Moss, and despite several attempts he would not come to her call. Retracing her steps, Miss Main then made her way onto the viaduct and crossed over to the Spey Bay side where she found Sandy and Jake discussing tactics for fishing in the high water.

'Hello Sandy,' said a slightly agitated Miss Main, 'you haven't seen Moss, my dog, have you?'

'He's a brown springer, is that right?' asked Jake. Miss Main nodded and Sandy was about to reply in the negative when Jake pointed to the opposite bank of the river.

'Is that him oer there?' Sylvia looked round just in time to see Moss, who had seen, and now wanted to join his mistress, jump into the fast-flowing Bridge Pool.

Robbie, Gonzo and the Stingman were down by the bottom of the Bridge Pool chasing a mink they had seen hanging around the netbox when they heard the shouts and looked up to see Moss being swept towards them, his nose poking out of the water as he struggled in vain against the strong current.

*

The story of Moss's rescue was the front page lead in that week's *Northern Scot*. Under the headline, 'Heroic Salmon Fishermen In Dramatic River Rescue' was a picture of the beaming Summer Crew petting a cheerful Moss who was looking up at a clearly-relieved Miss Sylvia Main.

'Listen te this,' said Jake, reading from the paper he had spread out on the top of the netbox.

> 'The three bold salmon fishermen waded out into the strongest part of the current to rescue the exhausted dog. Said Miss Sylvia Main, 39, "Moss is the most important thing in my life, and if it hadn't been for the brave actions of the salmon fishing crew, he would have been taken from me. I don't know how to thank them enough."'

'I can think of a wey,' said the Neap suggestively. Robbie reached over and clipped him round the ear.

'That's enough o that ye derty little rat...that's nae wey to speak aboot a nice wifey like Miss Main. And if ye say ony-thing mair, ye'll get a clip roon the ither lug.'

'It'd bring a tear te a gless ee,' said Corbie, unconsciously echoing the thoughts of Mr R M Mackintosh who strongly suspected that 'Scoop' Shand had deliberately exaggerated the bravery of the Summer Crew as a way of making him look stupid in front of the Amenities Committee.

That evening, however, Mr R M Mackintosh's mood was lightened when he took his dog Sweep for his custom-ary walk over the viaduct where he noticed that the heavy rain and wind of previous days had flattened large sections of the barley in George's field, effacing the obscenity, and thereby removing the stain from the good name of the village. Though George was less happy when he saw that he'd lost quarter of a field of barley.

The Laird's Wife

WHEN SANDY GEDDES, skipper of the Summer Crew, pulled up outside the bothy he found his first mate, Robbie, lying underneath his motorbike, fiddling with the engine, surrounded by the rest of the Summer Crew who were enjoying that most universal of pleasures – watching someone else work.

'Och, yer new bike's nae raxxed aridy is it, Robbie?' asked Sandy, as he joined the crowd around the motorbike.

'Aye,' said Robbie sheepishly, 'it conked oot aboot hauf a mile afore the turnoff, I hid te push it aa the wey here and I canna get it te start,' said Robbie, sitting up and wiping his oily hands on the grass.

'Weel, dinna look at me, I kaen nithing aboot ingines,' said Sandy.

'The werst o it is that I'm needin te get awa early the nicht,' said Robbie ruefully.

'Oh aye, fit are ye deeing?' asked Jake.

'Och nithing,' replied Robbie vaguely.

'Uh huh,' said Jake immediately picking up on Robbie's evasion, 'and faur aboots are ye deeing nithing?' Robbie, realising his mistake, looked up at Jake and, after a brief pause for thought, decided that a quick confession would probably be less painful in the long run.

'OK, if ye mist kaen, I'm gan oer te Sylvia Main's fur ma tea the nicht.'

'Sylvia Main fa runs the newsagent in Germouth?' asked Jake, feigning innocence.

'Fa's dug ye saved fae drooning?' added the Neap, joining in the fun.

'The verra same,' said Robbie, silently cursing his own stupidity, 'but it's early days yet. So dinna go spreadin it aroon.'

'So fit are ye g'te dee? Taak her oot fur a hurl on the back o the CB200?' asked Jake looking at the motorbike, 'thon thing's nae muckle yees fur courting.'

'Dinna be stupid,' said Robbie, frowning.

'A ton-up doon the Barmuckity straight, then oer the Dramlichs,' said the Neap revving an imaginary throttle. Fortunately for Robbie, he was saved further abasement at the hands of his fellow crew members by the arrival of a Blue/Grey Land Rover Defender 90 with a soft top and a rod rack, which appeared through the trees and parked by the bothy.

*

'Sandy, how are you?' asked the Laird as he and his wife stepped out of the Land Rover.

'Oh aye, fine thank you,' said Sandy, slightly flustered by

the sudden appearance of one of the most significant land-owners on the lower Spey, 'err, we were just helping Robbie with his bike; it's broken down.'

'Don't worry, I'm not here checking up on you...we're just here for a spot of fishing,' said the Laird with a kindly smile, as he and his wife released their salmon rods from the rack on the Land Rover.

The Laird was a tall, thin diffident man, whose close-set eyes, large ears and weak chin hinted at a too-shallow ancestral genepool. His wife, on the other hand, was a strikingly beautiful woman: tall and lean-limbed, her long, flame-red hair spilled over broad, athletic shoulders. Indeed, of the two, she was the one with aristocratic bearing, despite the fact that she'd been born the only daughter of an Anglican parson in one of London's more anonymous suburbs.

The Laird met his wife while she was playing a small role in a film partly shot on his estate, and, after a brief affair, the Laird, who was ten years her senior, divorced his first wife and married the actress, who had since thrown herself with great aplomb into the role which she had always suspected she was destined to play.

'Yes, we're going to fish the pools above the Bridge this morning, we thought it would make a change,' said the Laird checking the cast on the end of his line. As he did a large grilse rose in the slack water down towards the bottom of the pool by the opposite bank. The Laird stepped forward purposely with his rod, then checked his stride and looked at his wife.

'Err, sorry Fiona...ladies first,' he said, then immediately looked like he rather regretted saying it.

The Laird's wife smiled a rather fixed smile and shook her

head, 'no, please you go first.' The Laird hesitated.

'No, really, go on, I insist,' said the Laird's wife. The Laird, clearly embarrassed that this was playing out in front of Sandy, decided it was best to take his wife's invitiation at face value and not prolong any debate.

The Bridge Pool was, at that point, one of the largest pools on the lower Spey and the far, bottom end was a long cast even for an expert fisherman. The Laird paid out a short length of line, then started to cast in earnest, however, it soon became apparent that, despite his best efforts, he didn't quite have the range, with every cast falling about ten feet short of the slack water by the other bank. The water at the top of the Bridge Pool was too deep to wade into, so he walked down the bank to the scap where the water was shallower and waded in there. Unfortunately, that meant he was now casting directly into what was a reasonably stiff westerly breeze which negated any advantage he gained from wading into the river. The fish rose again, however, the Laird's cast again fell some way short. The Summer Crew, who had long since abandoned Robbie's mechanical troubles in favour of this new entertainment, quietly speculated whether he would make it. The consensus was that he wouldn't, and it wasn't long before the consensus was proven correct.

As the Laird wound in his line he turned and spoke to Sandy.

'I'll have to leave that one for you and the boys, Sandy,' he said smiling slightly awkwardly.

'Sorry, excuse me dear, but don't I get a go?' said the Laird's wife fixing him with the same strained grin, before turning to Sandy and smiling an altogether more friendly smile.

'I'm Fiona by the way, pleased to meet you,' she said, proffering her hand. Sandy hesitated, then took it and shook it.

'Oh, sorry Fee, I meant to introduce you, I didn't realise you two hadn't...' said the Laird apologetically as his wife picked up her rod and walked to the top of the pool, ignoring her husband.

With a few lazy flicks of her wrist the Laird's wife had the fly halfway across the pool, then she switched to a Spey cast: a casting technique developed on the lower beats of the Spey that keeps the fly and line from travelling behind the person casting, and helps not only avoid snagging obstacles on the bank behind, but can also extend the distance of a cast. The Spey cast can be hard to master, however, in the hands of an expert, which the Laird's wife clearly was, it is a thing of great beauty, and the Summer Crew watched transfixed as her line flew through the air and danced across the water as if she were spelling out some ancient incantation over the unsuspecting fish before she released the line with one final flourish and landed the fly exactly at the top of the slack water with what seemed like impossible delicacy and precision. Even Corbie was impressed.

The fish didn't take on the first cast, so the Laird's wife cocked her wrists and flicked out another perfect cast back to the top of the slack water again, and then three times more, until the fish struck.

As the Laird's wife knelt on the scap dispatching the ten pound grilse, she looked up, smiled and apologised.

'Sorry for taking your catch, Sandy,' she said.

'Not to worry; plenty more fish in the sea, as they say,' replied Sandy.

'Yes, thanks Sandy, and we'll get out of your way now,

sorry to be wasting your time,' said the Laird clearly keen to be elsewhere.

'Weel,' said Jake, turning to Robbie as the Laird and his wife walked off over the viaduct, deep in conversation, 'noo ye see fit a fash wumen can be. It's nae oer late to cry it off wi Sylvia the nicht.'

*

'OK, boys, this is neither catching fish nor mending nets. Let's get a wee shotty in,' said Sandy later that afternoon to the crew who were standing by the netbox watching an otter fording the brae at the bottom of the Bridge Pool. As Sandy spoke, the Laird and his wife walked into the clearing by the bothy, and, as both were laughing, he surmised that they had patched up their differences.

'How was the fishing?' asked Sandy as the Laird shrugged off his tackle bag.

'Very good, we caught three grilse, one just over 12 pounds...' said the Laird deploying the collective pronoun in a somewhat opaque manner, 'how about you?'

'OK, a bit slow...but we're just off now to have a shot,' replied Sandy as the Laird turned and slipped his rod into the rack on the Land Rover.

'Oh really,' said the Laird's wife, 'do you mind if we stay to watch? I've never seen the salmon crew in action before...'

'Fine by me,' said Sandy, 'we're used to an audience on the netting.'

Twenty minutes later the Laird and his wife stood arm-in-arm on the scap watching the Summer Crew as they hauled in the net.

'So what did you get?' asked the Laird's wife when they

were finished.

'Two grilse, a couple of sea trout and a finnock,' said Sandy scratching his head, disappointed that they hadn't landed a slightly more impressive catch, 'it's not been a great year for the fish.' The Laird nodded and smiled.

'Catches are down everywhere...though that sea trout looks splendid,' he said, 'and I'm a firm believer that they make better eating than the salmon.'

'Aye, I've heard that said before,' said Sandy looking down at the meagre catch.

'You don't agree?' asked the Laird's wife.

'No, no, it's not that. It's just that I really don't know...I don't eat fish.'

'Really?' asked the Laird's wife incredulously, 'you've never even eaten salmon?'

'Aye, I had salmon once when I was younger, but I didn't like it much.'

'Remarkable,' she said turning to her husband with eyebrows raised.

*

'Do you mind if I have a look?' asked the Laird's wife as she, her husband, and Sandy walked past the bothy on their way back up to the Land Rover.

'No, come on, darling we've taken up enough of Sandy's time as it is,' said the Laird.

'You don't mind if I have a quick look in the bothy, do you, Sandy?' said the Laird's wife looking Sandy directly in the eye and leaving Sandy in no doubt that it would be in his best interests if he didn't.

'Of...of course,' said Sandy, holding the door open, 'but

I'm sorry that it's not very, er, you know…well, it could do with a woman's touch, let's just say that.'

'What do you mean?' asked the Laird's wife turning to face Sandy.

'Tidying up and what have you. To make it nice.'

'Because that's what women do?'

'No, no, I never meant that, I jist…'

'Oh Sandy, you must take no notice of my wife,' said the Laird with a nervous laugh, 'if she had her way this country would be like Bolshevik Russia: with women down the pits and in the foundries.'

'If you want a woman's touch then you should employ a woman on the salmon crew,' the Laird's wife said to Sandy, ignoring her husband's interjection.

'Yes, well, it's not really…well it's not…' said Sandy struggling to think of a way out of this tight corner.

'What? It's not a woman's job. Is that what you were going to say?' asked the Laird's wife.

'No…' said Sandy flushing red.

'Well, Sandy's right…' said the Laird, now visibly annoyed, 'my god, Fiona, sometimes you can be impossible. Salmon fishing is man's work.'

'Rubbish. A woman could easily do this job,' said the Laird's wife coolly.

'Well, that's your opinion…' said the Laird dismissively, 'anyway, we must be going…thanks again Sandy and we'll see you anon.'

'No, no, wait a second,' said the Laird's wife, 'don't patronise me, I'm willing to put my money where my mouth is. I'll wager £50 that I can hold my own on one of the oars.'

*

'OK, boys I telt her that I'd run it by ye,' said Sandy looking over in the direction of the Laird and his wife, who were engaged in a low-volume, clenched-teeth kind of argument of which there was only going to be one winner.

'Fit's that?' asked Jake.

'The Laird's wife is needin te row an oar on a shot.'

When the commotion had died down, Sandy reminded the Summer Crew of the political expediencies of the situation.

'Nivir, it's nae chancey haeing a wifey on a boat,' said Robbie forcefully, 'if she gets on thon boat, there'll be hell te pey.' Fishermen are, as noted earlier, a superstitious bunch, and perhaps the strongest of all the superstitions was the fear of having a woman on board a fishing boat.

'Robbie, it's only a coble,' said the Stingman.

'Fit de you kaen aboot it,' said Robbie, sharply, 'boys hiv been killed on the salmon fushing afore. You've seen fit it's like fan the watter's up. I'm tellin ye, it's nae chancey haeing a wifey on board. It's bad luck. You see, this'll end in disaster...'

'I'm nae saying yer wrang, Robbie,' said Sandy, stroking his chin as he looked over at the Laird's wife, 'but I'd say it might go worse fur us if we refuse her.'

'But the Laird disna wint it te happen,' said Corbie.

'Aye, but he's nae the een wearing the widers in that marriage,' observed Jake.

*

'OK, so who am I rowing with?' asked the Laird's wife, as

she pulled on the thigh length black waders worn by all the crew; Sandy's views having prevailed despite Robbie and Corbie's reservations.

'What about the tall fellow?' said the Laird, glaring at his wife.

'Robbie?' said Sandy, looking over at his first mate, who talking animatedly to Corbie.

'A remarkable specimen,' said the Laird's wife thoughtfully, as she looked at Robbie's huge frame.

'Aye, I wouldn't want to be paying his food bills, that's for sure,' said Sandy.

'But I'm not rowing with him,' said the Laird's wife emphatically, 'it's not fair, there's not another man in Moray, maybe even the whole of the North, who could row with him if he put his mind to it. What about his partner?'

'The Nea…oh Neil…well, I'm sure that would be fine,' said Sandy desperately trying to calculate the outcome of the match and the possible and desirable consequences.

*

The shot with the Laird's wife was an odd affair: Sandy skipped the boat and let off the net while she and the Neap rowed; Jake, Corbie and Gonzo held the net on the bank. Meanwhile, Robbie, whose place she had taken, tried to fix his motorbike up by the bothy, still very unhappy that Sandy had consented to allow a woman on the boat.

Perhaps unsurprisingly, it turned out that the Laird's wife was more than up to the task, easily keeping up with the rowing and manfully, if that's the correct term, hauling the nets. When they'd finished, she led the crew back up to the bothy where they found Robbie still trying to fix his motorbike.

'What's wrong with your bike?' she asked, as she boxed the two fish she had carried up from the river by the gills.

'I'm not sure,' mumbled Robbie, looking up at her.

'Can I have a look?' she asked. Robbie looked at her suspiciously. 'I drove a motorbike across America once, I know a little bit about them,' she continued. Robbie stood up and made a gesture towards the bike as if to say 'be my guest.' The Laird's wife smiled then squatted down by the engine.

'It could be the float bowls...but maybe...have you tried the petcock?' she asked after a couple of minutes poking around. Robbie shook his head.

'There's no fuel getting down to the carburettor, which could mean it's got some gunk in it,' she said, half to herself, as she rolled up her sleeves and reached for Robbie's tools.

Fifteen minutes later the Laird's wife sat on Robbie's bike, revving the throttle. It was running perfectly.

*

'Well, Sandy, it's been an interesting day,' said the Laird, 'thank you, for, err..being so understanding.' And he was about to start the Land Rover, when he suddenly remembered something.

'Sandy, dash it, I almost forgot, here are the tickets for the Summer Garden Party, it's half the reason we came down...I hope we'll see you all there,' said the Laird fishing a sealed envelope out of the glovebox of the car and handing it to Sandy through the window.

'Aye weel, Cinderella, it looks like ye wull be able te gan te the ball, efter aa,' said Jake to Robbie, as the Land Rover drove off up the track to the main road.

The Keith Show

THE SEA HAAR that had kept the Summer Crew cool for the early shift burned off just before lunch, and it had turned into a broiling hot afternoon on the Spey. As soon as the shift ended, the three younger crew members stripped off to their boxer shorts and jumped into the Bridge Pool to escape the heat; Sandy, Robbie and Jake sat in the shade on the bench by the viaduct and watched them swim as they waited for Brian to come and pick up the fish.

'Are ye nae coming in fur a dook, Robbie?' asked Gonzo, who was treading water at the edge of the current.

'No, no,' said Robbie, shaking his head.

'That's because he canna swim,' said the Neap who was now sunning himself on one of the large, flat rocks by the river.

'Is that right?' asked the Stingman who was standing in the water on a rock.

'Maist o the auller fishers canna swim...Robbie, Sandy, Jake...even Brian, the skipper o the permanent crew; he sailed roon the world ten times on the merchant boats and he canna swim,' said the Neap.

'And he canna skipper a salmon boat either,' muttered Robbie.

'Aye, but he'll show these loons a hing or twa next wik, will he?' said Jake clapping his hands together.

'How's that?' asked Gonzo lifting himself out of the river and joining the Neap on the hot rocks by the edge of the Bridge Pool.

'It's the Keith Show,' said Robbie, 'aa the permanent members of the crew get the day off. It's Brian's turn te stay ahind and skipper the Summer Crew this year. And ye'll nae get an easy ride fae him. He's a Navy man. He'll stand nane o yer nonsense, ye'll be saluting and scrubbing the decks, and if ye dinna toe the line, ye'll get a taste o the cat or mebbe even keelhaaled.'

'Aye, weel mebbe that's true, but we aa kaen fit ye'll be deein' up at the Keith Show,' said the Neap.

'Fit's that?' asked Robbie suspiciously.

'Eyeing up the yows,' said the Neap, slipping off his rock into the river to evade any potential retribution from Robbie.

'Aye well, that's rubbish for a start, because if ye mist kaen I'm nae even gan te the Keith Show,' said Robbie, 'I'm dee-ing ma motorbike test in Fochabers. It wis the only date I could get.'

*

The Keith Show, which takes place in August every year, is

one of the largest and most prestigious agricultural shows in Scotland. Like most agricultural shows, the Keith Show is a much anticipated occasion that not only gives farmers the opportunity to show their animals and do a bit of business, but also allows them to catch up and socialise with their friends and acquaintances. And though the show had nothing to do with the salmon fishing, the permanent members of the crew, like many estate workers, got the day off.

On the morning of the first day of the Keith Show, Sandy woke to find that the good weather had held and, after breakfast, he and his wife Meg got the bus up to Keith and walked up to the show ground. After watching the Elgin Round Table take on and beat the Huntly Young Farmers in the opening heat of the 'It's a Knockout' competition in the main ring, Meg met up with her friend Mintie and they went off to watch the Highland Dancing, leaving Sandy to nip into the town to buy some pipe tobacco. Sandy was exiting the newsagent on Mid Street when the familiar figure of Robbie, wearing a yellow bib over his leather jacket, drew up on his new bike.

'Fit are you deeing here?' asked Sandy, surprised to see his first mate ten miles away from where he was supposed to be taking his bike test.

'Weel, I'm nae quite sure te be honest wi ye,' said Robbie looking perplexed, 'the boy fa wis deeing the test telt me te taak a right, then anither een, then anither een. But I think I got a wee bitty mixed up.'

'Wis he following ye on his bike?'

'No, he wis standing in the square wi a clipboard.'

'Are ye sure he didna jist want ye te gan roon the square?' speculated Sandy. Robbie thought for a moment, trying to recall the examiner's exact instructions.

'Aye, I suppose he mist of,' he said shaking his head, 'I wis wondering hoo he wid kaen if I wis ony guid if he couldna see me.'

Sandy shook his head.

'Och weel, I suppose I've failed ma test then, hiv I?' asked Robbie looking despondent. Sandy nodded, 'I'd say there wis a fair chance. Fit are ye g'te dee?'

'I dinna kaen, but I suppose I micht as weel maak the best o it and jine ye at the show,' said Robbie looking a little brighter.

'Aye, but wull the boy nae be still staunin there looking fur ye?'

'Naw,' said Robbie, looking at his watch, 'I dinna think so, he said he hid anither test te dee in Elgin, which wis aboot noo. I dinna think he wid've hung aroon.'

*

'I couldna be a fermer,' ruminated Robbie, leaning on the side of a pen of Blackface sheep, 'look at em...they're feil, and then there's aa the dubs and sharn....naw, jist gie me a net in ma haun and ah'm happy....there's a wee bitty excitement iviry time ye cast a net, kaen. Faur's the excitement looking efter thon glaikit baests? I mean dinna get me wrang, ferming's a teuch job like, and I've got ivry respect fur the boys fit dis it, but it's nae fur me.' Sandy nodded his head, looking distracted.

'Ye're awfa quiet, fit's awrang?' asked Robbie.

'I'm jist a wee bitty concerned aboot the boat.'

'Och, dinna be silly, Brian'll get them whipped in te shape.'

'That's fit I'm concerned aboot, ye kaen fit the young

loons is like. It could be a recipe fur disaster.'

'Sandy, we're on wer holidays, let's gan te the beer tent and see fit the crack is, forget aboot the fushing.'

'OK, I suppose yer right,' said Sandy.

'That's guid,' said Robbie, 'noo, I wis g'te ask if ye widna tell the boys aboot fit happened the day. It's a wee bitty embarrassing, and ye kaen fit they're like...I'd nivir hear the end o it.'

'OK,' said Sandy, 'seeing as yer buying.'

*

In fact, Sandy's concerns about the state of relations between Brian and the Summer Crew couldn't have been further from the mark; both parties had been on good terms ever since Brian turned up first thing that morning driving the tractor with the coble on the back.

'Richt boys, we're shootin doon fae the Quarry Pool the day,' said Brian, waving them up onto the trailer, instructions which were well received as shooting down the river from one pool to the next meant no hauling and a welcome change of scenery. And, as the morning wore on, it became apparent that Brian's regime was almost the exact opposite of that predicted by Robbie; indeed, it was so easy going that, by the time they pulled onto the shore of their customary lunch spot on the Gow's Island, the Summer Crew had only managed two shots instead of the usual five or six.

The Gow's Island was the largest and most inaccessible of all the islands and braids on the lower part of the Spey. Surrounded by wide channels of fast flowing water six feet deep on either side, the stony northern end was the nesting ground for the gulls and terns which gave the island its name, while the southern end of the braid was a sun trap, sheltered from the birds' perpetual squabbling by a stand of whins and gorse.

'Yer taakin it awfa easy the day, Brian,' said Corbie, lying back on the soft grass.

'Weel, seeing as the ithers are awa enjoying themselves, I dinna see why we should braak oor backs. In fact, I dinna see why we shouldna hae a wee dram,' said Brian producing a bottle of whisky from the small canvas satchel in which he kept his sandwiches. The Summer Crew needed no second invitation to join him and between the six of them they finished the bottle in fifteen minutes, with Brian taking Jake's share.

'Hey, Gonzo, ye've nae got ony o thon "wacky backy" hiv ye?' asked Brian, as he finished the last of the whisky. Gonzo looked at the Stingman and shrugged.

'Oh, dinna worry,' said Brian, 'I'm nae looking te cause ye trouble. I've smoked it afore, fan I wis in Casablanca wi the Merchant Navy. I wis jist thinking it wid be fine te hae a wee puff the noo.'

Brian took three long puffs on the joint and passed it on to Corbie who shook his head.

'Come on man, it'll help chill ye oot,' said Brian.

'Nae chance, I dinna want te turn in te some sort o hippy,' said Corbie, looking at the joint suspiciously.

'Weel boys, I dinna kaen fit Sandy and Robbie are up te at the Keith Show, but I'd say we've got the best o it here,' said Brian laying back in the soft green grass and slipping his hands behind his head.

Ironically, while the Summer Crew were enjoying themselves, their skipper, who was supposed to be relaxing, was most certainly not.

'Noo,' said Robbie expanding on his thoughts about the merits of the farming way of life, 'it's nae that I've got onything against fermers, but it's jist that the eens I kaen are aye gan on aboot fit diseases their baests hiv got. That's aa they spik aboot. That and the price o feed.'

'Aye, but it wid be fine to hae some land o yer ain,' said Sandy, 'ye'll aye be werking for someone else on the inshore boats, and if the catches keep gan doon there micht nae be ony nets soon enough...' said Sandy staring gloomily at the foamy map on the top of his half drunk pint.

'Sandy, ye need to stop fretting, the fishing is nae ge te finish jist because yer nae there fur a day,' said Robbie.

'I canna help it. I canna enjoy masel. I canna help thinking that it's g'te end badly wi Brian and the young loons.'

*

'This is alright,' said the Stingman, looking over at Brian who lay snoring loudly in the hot sun.

'Aye, but ye kaen hoo he's actin like this?' said Jake quietly.

'Because he wants us to like him. It's a bit sad really, but we're not complaining,' said Gonzo quietly.

'Aye weel, mebbe that's pairt o it, but I'd say it's got mair te dee wi the bet him and Sandy hiv aboot fit crew catches maist fush in the season. If we catch next te nithing the day, then it's pits us even further ahind...'

Brian woke an hour later, to find his only company was the bickering gulls, for he had been marooned by his crew on the Gow's Island. And as, like the rest of the older salmon fishers, he couldn't swim, there was no escape.

Three hours later, the Summer Crew, skippered by Jake,

were boxing their last shot when Brian appeared marching down the bank towards the viaduct, having been rescued from the island by a passing ghillie.

'Here he is; Papillion himsel,' said Jake quietly as Brian approached.

'He looks like he's cocht the sun a wee bitty,' said Corbie.

'He's like a Baxter's beetroot,' said Jake, and the rest of the Summer Crew were still laughing as Brian reached them.

'Ye'll nae be laughing in half an oor's time fan I've got the hale lot o ye sackit, that wis mutiny, nithing less,' he said, his eyes full of the wrath he'd nursed on the Gow's Island.

'Aye, and fan you're doon at Tugnet, mebbe ye'll explain te Neil's faither fit ye smoked efter ye hid yer piece, Captain Bligh,' said Jake, looking over at the Neap.

*

The next morning, Sandy arrived at the bothy to find Jake leaning against the netbox reading the paper.

'Did ye hae a guid day at the Keith Show?' asked Jake, as Sandy unlocked the coble.

'Aye, it wis fine.'

'Did onything mich happen?'

Sandy shook his head.

'Nae really. Fit aboot here?' he asked, standing up stiffly.

'No, it wis a quiet day, Brian hid us working herd, we cocht fair few fush, but that wis aboot it.'

Lord Possilpark's Lucky Shot

A FEW DAYS AFTER the Keith Show, the Summer Crew were getting ready for the first shot of the day when their skipper, Sandy Geddes, approached the three younger members with a proposition.

'Boys, fan I wis doon the icehooses earlier on, I seen the Super and he telt me that the Laird has asked him for a len o some boys fur a three-day grouse shoot starting on the 12th. Div ye fancy it?' The Stingman looked at Gonzo and shrugged.

'It's up te yersels,' continued Sandy, 'but it's guid money seeing as it's on tap o yer salmon pey, and ye'll get bed and board in een o the shooting bothies.'

'What would you do about running the boat?' asked the Stingman.

'We'll get Ian Masson fae the permanent crew and run short-handed for the Thursday and Friday, and we're nae here on the Seturday…'

'What's the beating like; have you done it afore?' asked Gonzo.

'Aye, fan I wis young and swack,' said Sandy with a rueful look down at his legs, 'but ma knees widna get up and doon thon braes nooadays, but it's guid fur a change, though.'

'Fit aboot it Neil, are ye keen?' The Neap looked uncertain.

'Yer nae feart o bit of exercise are ye?' said Corbie who'd wandered over to join them.

'No, I'm nae Corbie, if ye mist kaen, I'm nae oer keen on the shooting, I canna understaun hoo people wint tae kill things fur fun.'

'Ye kill the fush iviry day,' said Corbie.

'Aye, but it's nae the same, I dinna enjoy it, and its nae fur fun, it's fur fowk te ate.' Corbie shook his head, clearly unsympathetic to the Neap's moral position.

'Och, come on Neil, it'll be a laugh,' urged Gonzo, 'you're nae pulling the trigger.'

*

August the 12th, otherwise known as 'the Glorious 12th' by the shooting fraternity, is the start of the grouse shooting season. Of course, it's possibly a less glorious day if you're a grouse, however, it is often argued by the shooting fraternity that if it wasn't for the careful management of the birds for the purpose of shooting there would be next to no grouse on the moors, and who knows, perhaps as they are blasted from the skies, the grouse are consoled by the knowledge that their individual sacrifice is for the greater good of their species. For who is to say what secrets lie in the soft, downy breast of a grouse?

Not that any such questions were on the mind of the three younger members of the Summer Crew as, a few days after Sandy's proposition, they sat among the flowering heather just below the summit of the Meikle Ben eating the blaeberries and cloudberries they found growing there while they watched the gamekeepers' dogs chase mountain hares through the peat hag. It was a beautiful, clear morning and looking northward, they could see right down to the mouth of the Spey and the Moray Firth; to the west, the Black Isle and Ben Wyvis; to the east, Benachie; and to the south, the tops of Ben Avon and other Cairngorms beyond.

'Aye weel, I wisna oer keen, but I'll admit this is nae bad,' said the Neap, lying back in the heather with the sun on his face.

Ten minutes later the Head Keeper got out of the Argocat, where he'd been on the walkie-talkie to the keeper organising the guns, and walked over to where the beaters were sitting.

The Head Keeper was a tall, lean, gruff man with piercing blue eyes and short cropped, sandy hair. Dressed in a three-piece, green tweed suit with plus twos, green canvas gaiters and on his feet a pair of highly-polished Hoggs of Fife boots. Looking down at the beaters he pushed his deerstalker hat back, scratched his forehead and leaned forward on the shepherd's crook he carried with him.

'Right, we're ready te go, but before we do there's three things ye need te know;

1. Keep in line;
2. Make plenty o noise; and
3. Stop when I blow the horn.

If ye do that, ye'll get nae trouble from me.'

*

The principle of a driven grouse shoot is simple. The guns, as the shooters are known, squat out of sight in a line of butts spaced evenly down the flank of a hill. Butts can be simple holes dug in the peat or rather more complicated and salubrious affairs with dry stone walls and wooden benches. When the guns are in place in the butts, the beaters are lined up, out of sight, down the far side of the hill. At the start of the drive the beaters walk forward round the hill and towards the butts waving flags made from hazel rods and old plastic fertiliser sacks, making as much noise as possible in order to scare the grouse over the butts, where they are, theoretically at least, shot by the guns lying in wait. When the beaters get to about fifty yards or so away from the butts, the Head Keeper blows his hunting horn and the guns turn around 180 degrees so that they do not hit the approaching beaters who then finish off the drive to the butts, with the guns only shooting birds driven over their shoulders. When the drive is finished, the guns and beaters are transported to another part of the hill where the process is repeated.

The first drive of that morning was fairly ragged, but the guns got a good bag so there were no complaints. The second drive was better executed, and, when the Head Keeper blew his horn, the beaters were more or less in a straight line. Having given the guns a couple of minutes to turn, the Head Keeper blew the horn a second time, signalling to the beaters that they should finish off the drive. The Stingman and Gonzo, who were beating next to one another, started forward, continuing their noisy debate about the merits of the Stone Roses' eponymous first album, when, about twenty yards from the butts, a grouse flew up chuckling with alarm. Suddenly, a gun in front of them exploded into life shooting in the wrong direction. Fortunately, the shot missed both of the salmon fishers who threw themselves into the heather as the shooter tried, and failed, to down the bird with his second barrel.

*

'He could have killed us,' said Gonzo indignantly to the Head Keeper.

'Look boys, I understand,' said the Head Keeper looking marginally less severe than usual, 'I've reminded the gun about which way to shoot and he's agreed to apologise and he's offering £20 for each of ye, as a token of his good will.' And though both the Stingman and Gonzo were unimpressed by the thought that their lives might be worth as little as £20 each, they didn't fancy disagreeing with the intimidating figure of the head keeper.

'Now, he wants to apologise personally,' continued the Head Keeper, 'but I'm warning ye now, thank him for his apology and leave it at that. He's a Lord of the Realm and a powerful man. So we dinna want to rock the boat. Is that clear?'

The Head Keeper, showing due deference, introduced the students to the man who had so nearly proved their nemesis – Lord McKay of Possilpark, the ex-shipyard riveter and union leader who had served briefly as a minister in Jim Callaghan's doomed Labour Government of the late

1970s before 'taking ermine' and completing his long political journey from the shipyards of Red Clydeside to the grouse moors of upper Speyside.

'Look boys, sorry aboot that, eh,' said Lord Possilpark, a corpulent man in his late sixties, whose huge belly was clear testament to his enjoyment of the finer things in life, 'ma eyes are no quite whit they used te be; know whit I mean?' he said, pointing to the large, square, 'jamjar' spectacles perched on the end of his bulbous, red nose.

'Now boys, here's a wee present te ye, te say ah'm sorry and let that be the end o it, eh,' he continued, as the Head Keeper handed the money to the Stingman and Gonzo who put it in their pockets.

'Ah'll hae a swally te that, eh,' said Lord Possilpark before taking a swig from the large green leather hip flask he held in his hand.

On the next beat the Stingman led the choir in a song he had learnt in order to impress a girl on a recent anti-Poll Tax march. Both he and Gonzo waved their plastic flags enthusiastically as they struggled through the heather, singing at the top of their lungs,

> 'The people's flag is deepest red,
> It shrouded oft our martyr'd dead
> And ere their limbs grew stiff and cold,
> Their hearts' blood dyed its ev'ry fold.
>
> Then raise the scarlet standard high,
> Within it's shade we'll live and die,
> Though cowards flinch and traitors sneer,
> We'll keep the red flag flying here.'

At lunchtime the guns took their places at a table that had been set up outside one of the shooting huts where they enjoyed, set out on a crisp white linen tablecloth, a lunch of hot beef consomme followed by cold snipe and potato salad with a *tarte framboises* to finish, all washed down with several bottles of 1er Cru Puligny-Montrachet, and some freshly brewed coffee. Some way up the hill the beaters sat in the heather with the dogs, eating their packed lunch, which consisted of a cheese roll, an apple and a bottle of Irn Bru, and watching the clouds roll over the foothills of the Cairngorms. As they finished their lunch and started to get ready for the next beat, Gonzo and the Stingman spotted the Labour peer in animated discussion with the Head Keeper, who five minutes later took them to one side.

'Right,' he said, grabbing the Stingman by the elbow and squeezing so hard it hurt, 'it has been brought to my attention that there's a number of you beaters singing a song which has offended several of the guns and embarrassed the man who was kind enough to give you a tip for your trouble this morning.' The Neap started laughing.

'What the hell are you laughing about?' asked the Head Keeper scowling at the Neap who shrugged.

'Anyway, this is the last warning, any more trouble from you lot and I'm going straight to the Laird. And he can get you taken off the salmon fishing.' The Neap giggled again.

'Do you think I'm joking, pal?' said the Head Keeper menacingly. The Neap shook his head and looked down. The Head Keeper, satisfied that he'd got his point across, turned to leave.

'Oh, aye and another thing,' he said, stopping and turning, 'no one calls anyone else comrade on ma grouse moor.

D'ye understand?'

'Why were you laughing?' asked the Stingman angrily, as the Head Keeper strode off to check the dogs. The Neap smiled, then pulled a large green leather hip flask from his pocket, put it to his lips and took several swift gulps.

'Is that…?' asked Gonzo. The Neap nodded.

'I fff, found it in the heather, he mm, mist of drapped it,' slurred the Neap.

'Gees a howp,' said Gonzo. The Neap handed over the hip flask, but it was empty, apart from a small dribble that Gonzo drank anyway.

'Woah, that's strong,' he said, wincing as he swallowed. The Stingman took the flask and sniffed the neck of the flask.

'Is that broonic?' he asked the Neap, who nodded again and hiccuped.

'How much have you had?' The Neap hiccupped again, but said nothing.

'Wis it full?' The Neap nodded. Drinking the full flask might not have been too much of a problem if the whisky hadn't been broonic: had it been full of standard strength whisky, he would have consumed no more than a normal quarter bottle, however, as it was broonic he'd drunk the equivalent of just over a normal half bottle in the space of about 20 minutes.

*

The Neap stood swaying gently in the light breeze. He hadn't said anything for about ten minutes, and the beat after lunch was about to start.

'What are we going to do with him?' asked the Stingman.

'I don't know...' said Gonzo.

'If the Head Keeper works out that he's plastered then he's likely to sack the lot of us.'

The first beat of the afternoon was a struggle, the Neap was all over the place, stumbling around and occasionally groaning, however, while that would raise eyebrows elsewhere, it's required behaviour for a grouse beater, so he attracted no undue attention. However, as the beaters lined up for the second beat the Neap was sick.

'Jist leave me here, I need a wee sleep, ma heid's spinning, and I'm needin it te stop,' he said as he curled up into a ball at the bottom of a peat hag.

'No, you just stick in between us,' said the Stingman, dragging the Neap to his feet, 'there's only one more beat to do, then we'll be back in the bothy, and you can sleep as much as you like.'

On the final beat of the day, the Stingman and Gonzo alternated taking turns holding the Neap upright as he stumbled across the hill, hoping that the Head Keeper wouldn't see them. It was a struggle, but as they neared the end of the beat the Stingman started to relax: it looked like they'd got away with it. However, just then a fox broke cover about ten yards in front of them, and ran towards the butts. The cry went up from one of the young keepers, 'A fox. A fox.' The guns stood up, eager to get a shot at it as it ran past them.

'No, nae the fox, dinna kill the fox, it nivir deen ye ony herm,' shouted the Neap, breaking free from the Stingman's grip and staggering towards the guns. Gonzo intercepted the Neap, however, as he tried to get a better grip of the Neap's jacket, he slipped and fell into a pool of bright green sphagnum moss. The Neap staggered onwards towards the guns, roaring drunkenly.

'I'm the fox, I'm the fox, shoot me,' he shouted as he veered along the line of butts, before tripping and falling onto his knees. The fall didn't stop him, however, and he scrambled along on his knees continuing to shout 'I'm the fox' at the top of his voice in a desperate attempt to distract the attention of the guns and save the fox.

A tactic which, for the most part worked, as the guns, startled by the behaviour of the Neap, lowered their weapons. All but one that was, who took aim and fired. The Stingman and Gonzo watched as the shot rang out and the Neap fell sidewards as if tugged over by a rope.

'I got him, I got him. I shot the fox,' shouted Lord Possilpark, who reached for a celebratory swig from his hip flask.

*

Fortunately for everyone concerned, Lord Possilpark's lucky shot had only sprayed a few pellets into the Neap's left buttock. As the Head Keeper drove the wounded and slightly freaked out Neap off the hill in the Argocat, Gonzo and the Stingman sought out Lord Possilpark, who they found pouring himself a brandy from another hip flask in one of the butts.

'Why did you shoot him?' asked Gonzo angrily.

'He said he was the fox,' said a confused Lord Possilpark, quickly downing the brandy and reaching for his wallet for a second time that day.

By the time he'd been admitted to Dr Gray's in Elgin, the Neap had started to sober up, and as the doctor cut the pellets from his behind, he vowed never to drink again, having learnt a valuable, though painful, lesson about the perils of drinking broonic.

As he sat in the waiting room the Head Keeper considered his options. He had been sorely tempted to sack all three of the Summer Crew on the spot, however, on reflection, he judged that the most sensible course of action was to avoid any further controversy and let the Stingman and Gonzo beat for the final two days of the shoot. He didn't want anyone getting wind of the fact that a beater had been shot by a guest, and besides, there was almost no chance of getting replacement beaters at such short notice.

A Portent

O N THE THIRD and final day of the grouse beating, the beaters, including Gonzo and the Stingman, stood with the keepers and dogs in the paved yard behind the old stable block of the Big Lodge, sheltering from the inclement weather which had blown in at the end of the second day. In fact, the weather had deteriorated to such an extent that the shooting party decided they would prefer to rough shoot for grouse rather than sit around in cold butts for the day.

In a rough, or walk-up shoot, parties of one or two guns, along with a gamekeeper, a dog handler and three or four dogs walk the moor, with the dogs running ahead flushing the grouse and then retrieving the dead birds.

'You're coming with me and the two Italian guns,' said the Head Keeper to the Stingman, who he now considered a troublemaker and at least partially to blame for the unfortunate shooting of the Neap two days before. 'I want to keep an eye on you,' he said gruffly.

Gonzo, meanwhile, was assigned to a serious looking German industrialist, with frameless designer spectacles and a very hi-tech carbon fibre shotgun. However, as the shooting party left the yard, the Laird's wife, a tall, striking woman in her mid-thirties dressed in tight, brown tweed plus fours, a Barbour jacket and a pair of green Hunter wellies, stopped him.

'I think you'd better come with me,' she said.

'Oh right, erm,' said Gonzo, looking over to where the Head Keeper was talking to one of the guns, 'it's just that he said I should go with the German guy.'

'Oh, don't worry about Francis, his bark is much worse than his bite, and besides, who do you think he works for?' Gonzo shrugged, 'OK, which keeper is coming with us? I'll go and get the dogs from him.'

'I don't need a keeper,' said the Laird's wife dismissively, 'I know these mountains like the back of my hand. All I need is a fit, young dog handler who can keep up with me Heathcliff and Rochester,' she said reaching down and petting the giant Deerhound and black and white Springer Spaniel which stood by her side.

'You are fit?' she said straightening up and looking directly at Gonzo.

'Er, yes, I suppose so, I've been on the salmon boats for two months.'

'Oh yes, I thought I recognised you. Anyway, that's good because there's a lot of money riding on this shoot you know.'

'Oh...right.'

'Yes, at dinner last night there were some very substantial wagers placed on whether my husband or I would bag most grouse today, and I have no intention of losing.'

*

At the start of the rough shoot, the Stingman, following the Head Keeper's instructions, held the black Lab on a lead, while the Springer Spaniel worked the moor ahead. Within less than fifty steps a yellow wagtail flew up from behind a tussock of grass. Instantly, both Italians shouldered their shotguns, letting off both barrels at the tiny bird, which disappeared in a puff of feathers. When the smoke had cleared, the Head Keeper tried to explain to the Italians, neither of whom spoke any English, that they couldn't shoot wagtails.

'No, no, no. Cannot shoot.'

'No, a, shoota?'

'Illegal, protected.'

'*Protteto?*'

'Yes, *si*, *protteto*,' said the Head Keeper, shaking his head as he turned to face the Stingman. 'These Italians, if it moves they'll shoot it. It's no right shooting a wagtail wi a shotgun.'

'If I say *protetto*. You no shoot. Understand?' said the Head Keeper turning back to the Italians to underline his point. The Italians nodded, but the Head Keeper spent much of the rest of the morning bellowing *protetto* at the Italians who still took aim when any bird, no matter how small, took to the wing.

*

The Laird's wife was an athletic woman and she set a stiff pace, quickly leading Gonzo and the dogs to near the top of the Meikle Ben, bagging several brace of grouse on the way. Just under the summit the Laird's wife stopped shooting and walked round to the Eagles' Crag. Standing on the edge of the 500 ft drop with the wind blowing in her hair, and her giant Deerhound by her side, she beckoned to Gonzo, indicating that he should join her by the precipice.

'It's so dramatic up here, don't you think?' she said, shouting to make herself heard above the roar of the wind. Gonzo, looked down and swallowed his fear.

'See how the rain sweeps up the valley. Up here you can appreciate the sublime and elemental forces of nature. Up here we are closer to the gods. Up here we are more alive.' Gonzo nodded and took a step back from the edge.

'No, you must embrace your fear. Step back to the edge and feel the wind rush past you,' said the Laird's wife, holding out her hand.

*

At around the same time, though somewhat lower down the hill, the Stingman, the Head Keeper and the Italians had stopped for lunch. As the Italians ate and chatted, the Head Keeper sat in silence.

'So how much of this does the Laird own?' asked the Stingman, pointing down the valley.

'As far as you can see to the east, and to the west…up to the river,' said the Head Keeper pouring himself a cup of tea from his flask.

'Really, he owns all of that?'

'Uh huh.'

'How much land do you own?' The Head Keeper looked up at the Stingman, but did not reply.

'That's not fair really, is it. I mean one man owning all this land,' continued the Stingman.

'His family have owned this land for centuries, and he's a good laird. They run the estate well. We could be owned by foreigners,' said the Head Keeper casting a derisive look at the Italians, 'folk who think it's aa right te shoot wagtails.'

*

As the Laird's wife and Gonzo finished their lunch the weather closed in, wreathing the top of the Meikle Ben in thick cloud, though this seemed to have little impact on the Laird's wife who, almost immediately, on the resumption of the shoot, bagged two more brace; one with a left, right shot.

'Did you see that,' said the Laird's wife with some pride, plucking a still-living grouse from the Springer Spaniel's mouth.

'Don't you think it's cruel killing all these animals?' asked Gonzo looking at the grouse.

'It's part of the cycle of life. Blood is spilt on the earth. Death is always near at hand...' said the Laird's wife calmly as she broke the neck of the quivering bird. After reaching round her back and slipping the grouse into the game bag she wore over her shoulder, the Laird's wife turned to move on just as a huge, white apparition rose up in the mist from the peat hag in front of them, then swept off over their heads.

'A snowy owl,' said the Laird's wife with a hushed voice as the bird dissolved into the swirling mist, 'a rare sight indeed. A portent perhaps.'

Meanwhile, the Head Keeper was beginning to regret his decision to take the Stingman along with him.

'But how can it be right that a handful of people own all the land in this country?'

'Look, this is not a political debate. This is a grouse shoot. And anyway, possession is nine tenths of the law.'

'No, but surely you must feel that it's unfair. You live in a tied cottage and do all the work, while the boss owns ten huge houses and swans around doing what he likes.'

'You should be here in the stalking season,' said the Laird's wife to Gonzo as they looked down on a group of hinds scenting the wind further down the hill, 'when the stags are in rut they are consumed, driven mad by their urge to procreate. Each bellowing wildly from hill to hill. Filling the valleys with their primal cries. It's so exhilarating. So life affirming.'

'Uh, huh,' said Gonzo, entirely unsure how to respond to these observations.

'Fighting for the right to mate with the hinds. To pass on their genes. Their blood. In the wild struggle for survival.'

'Well, I agree they should tax the very rich more,' said the Head Keeper, watching the Italians as they walked up the middle of the large peat hag near the top of the Meickle Ben that the stalkers called the Motorway.

'Yeah, but you know as well as I do,' said the Stingman, 'that they just leave the country or find some loophole. No, the only way forward is to confiscate all the big estates and hand the land back to the people.'

'Don't be ridiculous, this is nae Soviet Russia,' said the Head Keeper turning to face the Stingman as behind him a shot rang out.

'And after they've mated, they wallow in the hag,' said the Laird's wife removing her jacket, 'it too is a most liberating experience. You must try it. Come on let's wallow in the hag.'

'Err, look, I mean, what about your bet with the Laird?'

'Oh, don't worry about that, he's as bad with a gun in his hand as he is with a rod in his hand or a woman in his bed. I've already bagged twice as many birds as he's ever shot in one day,' replied the Laird's wife as she removed her jacket, then started to unbutton her blouse.

*

The Stingman and the Head Keeper knelt over the dead snowy owl. The Stingman leaned over to touch the bird.

'Look, it's tagged,' said the Stingman looking at the red ring on the bird's leg. As he ran his hand over the soft, white feathers, a lump formed in his throat and he had to look away as tears welled up in his eyes.

'Aye, they're very rare,' said the Head Keeper softly, 'I hate to see such a thing shot.'

'You should do something about it,' said the Stingman angrily.

'I'll lose my job if anyone finds out about this. It'll be me gets the blame for this dead bird no him,' said the Head Keeper looking over at the short Italian with the glasses, 'and nothing'll happen to him; he runs half their country.'

'It doesn't stop you telling him what's right and wrong on your moor,' said the Stingman, blowing his nose on a piece of tissue he found in his pocket.

The Head Keeper looked at the Stingman and took a

deep breath, then got to his feet and let the Italian guns have it with both barrels, and though they didn't understand much of what he said, they were left in no doubt what he felt about the dead bird.

Fifteen minutes later, as the Stingman, the Italians and the Head Keeper rounded the corner of a particularly incised peat hag on their way back down the hill, they were all astonished to find the Laird's wife *in flagrante delicto* with Gonzo, both of them naked and smeared in peat. The short Italian with the glasses turned to the Head Keeper.

'*Protetto?*' he asked, an ironic smile playing on his lips as he looked at Gonzo and the Laird's wife. The other Italian turned to his friend and smiled.

'*Non, cornutto,*' he said.

*

'You know that I could tell the Laird about what his wife and your pal were up to today,' said the Head Keeper to the Stingman as the Italians got out of the Land Rover and walked over to the Big Lodge, 'you boys from the salmon nets have caused me nothing but trouble for these three days.'

The Stingman reached into his pocket and pulled out the red metal tag he had removed from the foot of the snowy owl.

'Aye, but maybe sometimes it's best to let sleeping dogs lie,' said the Stingman putting the red metal tag on the dashboard and getting out of the Land Rover.

The Poachers

THE END OF the summer salmon fishing season on the River Spey was traditionally prefaced by the Laird's Summer Garden Party, one of the biggest events in the Morayshire summer social calendar, and though the salmon fishers weren't exactly among the county's elite they were all invited by dint of some half-remembered feudal obligation. Which is why the Neap, Gonzo, the Stingman, and Robbie were all sat in the cab of the pickup, dressed in their Sunday best, watching Corbie make his way up the path from his cottage.

'Robbie, how come you're not going to the dance with Sylvia?' asked the Stingman.

'I am, she's aff getting ridy wi her sister in Fochabers; I'll see her at the dunce,' replied Robbie looking in the mirror behind the sun visor and patting his head in an attempt to tame an unruly tuft of his spiky black hair.

'Fit like, Corbie?' continued Robbie, as Corbie opened the back door of the pickup, 'yer looking a hoor o a smert wi yer suit on.'

'The same as I aye dee,' said Corbie indignantly, 'onywey, come on, budge up, wer late.'

Five minutes later, as they drove up the road to Fochabers, a car parked down by the Essil pool caught the Stingman's attention. It had been driven in behind a stand of gorse, but was still just visible from the road.

'Did ye see that car?' asked the Stingman, sitting up and pointing towards the river.

'See fit?' asked Robbie who was sitting in the front passenger seat. 'Look, over by the river,' said the Stingman, 'there, there behind those bushes down by the Essil Pool.'

'Yes, yes, I see it, it's brown,' said Gonzo, leaning over and peering into the trees.

'That's poachers,' said Robbie thoughtfully, 'I wis spikkin te aull Hector the ghillie yisterday and he said that there wis a gang working Essil last wik. It'll be the same boys.'

'What are we going to do?' asked the Stingman.

'We shouldna dee onything,' said Corbie, 'we've got te get te the dunce, it's nithin te dee wi us.'

'And let the poachers taak the breed oot o oor moo?' said Robbie.

'Och no, Robbie, I'm nae getting inta a rammy wi some poachers fan I've got ma Sunday best on,' said the Corbie.

'Neil, turn in by the Essil pool at the next turnoff,' said Robbie sternly, 'or, fan we get te the dunce I'll gan straight te yer faither and tell him that ye drove on.'

'Could we nae jist stop at the next phone box and ca the bailiffs?' said Corbie.

'Ye kaen as weel as thon poachers dee that the bailiffs is aa at the dunce. That's why they're as brazen as te be oot afore it's dark. And onywey, the poachers'll maist likely be awa afore onybidy could get doon here.'

'Robbie, come on. It's nae wise getting inta a rammy wi the poachers,' said the Neap, 'fa kaens fit'll happen.'

The Neap was right, for while the poacher remains a romantic figure in Scottish folklore, and there are still plenty of salmon of 'uncertain provenance', caught by locals, lying curled among the bags of runner beans at the bottom of Morayshire's chest freezers, most of the poachers who worked the Spey by the end of the 1980s were part of professional criminal gangs, up from the central belt of Scotland. Men who would stop at nothing to get the fish, including poisoning the river with chemicals like Cymag or attacking the water bailiffs – the men who police the river – with baseball bats and knives. Indeed, poaching gangs had become so violent that the water bailiffs were, by that point, almost all ex-servicemen trained to deal with violence and personal attacks.

'Fit if there's a hale gang o them?' said the Neap anxiously, as he turned into the stand of Sitka spruce which ran down to the river.

'Dinna worry aboot that. Jist honk the horn, and let em kaen we're comin. They'll nae hing aroon. And if they dee – they'll wush they hidna,' said Robbie belligerently thumping his giant fist into his free hand.

Unfortunately, Robbie's first prediction proved incorrect, and as the Neap drew up at the gate by the river the four men who were standing there walked towards the pickup.

Robbie opened his door and jumped out to meet them.

'Fit are ye deein here?' he asked, loudly. The man at the back of the small group stepped forward.

'The Stot,' whispered the Neap quietly to no one in particular.

'Fit like Robbie, fine evening, ye look a wee bitty oer dressed fur the fushin,' said the Stot in a nonchalant, rather mocking manner.

'OK Peter, this is nae time fur nonsense, I'll gie ye a chance. Leave the fush faur they are, and drive aff, and I say nithing aboot this te the water balliffs.'

'Mind the last time we met, fan I skelped ye? Ae punch wis aa it took…and I wis stotious as weel…'

'Aye, fuck aff, or ah'll break yer fuckin kneecaps after he's beaten the shite oot o ye,' said a tall, thin man with a Glaswegian accent who stepped forward and pointed an axe handle in Robbie's direction.

The Stingman looked at Gonzo, who in turn looked at Corbie. It was, however, the Neap who was first to react, jumping out and running to Robbie's side.

'Come on then, I'll hae the hale jing bang lot o ye,' shouted the Neap, swinging the jack handle he'd grabbed from the floor of the pick up. The tall man halted and looked round at the Stot. Corbie, Gonzo and the Stingman followed the Neap out of the cab.

'Nae the noo, Neapy, this is atween me an Robbie…we'll sort this oot,' said the Stot taking off his jacket.

'Ma name's nae Neap, it's Neil.'

'Fit ivir, staun back, this is atween me and him.'

Robbie nodded at the Neap and slipped out of his suit jacket. As he did the Stot lunged at him, then feinted to the left swinging a right hook at Robbie's head. This time, however, Robbie was ready for him, deftly stepping back as the Stot swung, leaving him flailing at thin air. Before the Stot had time to regain his balance Robbie moved in and landed a straight left to the Stot's nose. The Stot staggered backwards slightly, blood streaming down his face, he swung again with his left, but he was dazed from Robbie's first punch and missed his target again. This let Robbie in for a second time. A left to the solar plexus, two heavy rights to the ribs, and another quick right to the temple knocked the Stot to his knees.

'Here take the hannel,' said the tall Glaswegian, offering the axe handle to the Stot.

The Stot, kneeling in the grass clutching his ribs and groaning slightly, looked at the axe handle and then up at Robbie.

'Go on, taak it Peter, but ye'll regret,' said Robbie towering over him.

And for a moment it seemed like the Stot might take it, but he was beaten and he knew it, so he slumped back down into the grass clutching his ribs and breathing heavily.

The tall Glaswegian man looked at Robbie, perhaps thinking he might have a try with the axe handle himself then, evidently thinking better of it, turned and joined the other two poachers as they ran towards the brown Ford Cortina parked in behind the bushes, leaving behind them a gill net and at least a couple of dozen fresh-caught grilse lying on it like constellations scattered across the heavens. As the poachers started the car, the Stot struggled to his feet and staggered, with some difficulty, over to the front passenger door. As soon as the Stot was in the car, the door slammed shut and it disappeared up the farm track in a cloud of dust.

*

'Thanks for the back up, Neil, I dinna mind saying I wis getting a wee bitty feart there, I thocht they were aa ge te jump me,' said Robbie, shaking the tension out of his arms.

'Aye,' said Corbie, 'they looked fairly roch kinda chiels.'

'Ye absolutely melled the Stot,' said the Neap, clearly in some awe of Robbie, 'that right te the heid.'

'They mist o heard his ribs cracking up in Aberlour fan you skelped him in the side,' said Corbie wincing slightly.

'I wonder what the rest of them made of us, all dressed in our suits,' said the Stingman.

'They probably thought we were the mafia,' said Gonzo.

'Or the best-dressed water bailiffs in the hale o Scotland,' said Corbie, as everyone laughed, expelling the nervous tension.

'Fit are we g'te de wi aa the fush?' asked the Neap when everyone had stopped laughing.

'Weel, we canna jist leave them for the gows,' said Robbie, 'we'll pit them in the back o the pick up.'

'Aye, but fit are we g'te de wi them efter?'

'We'll taak them doon te the ice hooses,' said Robbie.

'Jist hud on a wee minity,' said Corbie, 'we're nae gieing thon fush back. We foond em. By rights they're oors.'

'Is that a legal opinion?' asked Robbie.

'It's finders, keepers,' said Corbie as categorically as if he were an advocate explaining an elementary point of law to a newly-appointed jury.

'Och in that case,' said Robbie holding his hands up, 'I'm sure if ye jist explain that te the Sheriff…'

'Look,' said Corbie, interrupting Robbie before he could say any more, 'there's nae need te be sarcastic; they coulda tain thirty mair fush oot o thon pool the nicht. If ye look at it that wey, even if we taak these fush fur wersels we've saved the Laird a hape o money. And besides, mind fit happened te oor broonic? This wid jist be taakin back fae the Stot fit is rightfully oors. These are nae the Laird's fush onymair, these are the Stot's fush, and we're jist taakin back fae him fit he owes us.'

Robbie said nothing for a minute, and then shrugged.

'OK, ye hae a point aboot the broonic, but we canna mention a werd o this te Sandy.'

*

Robbie found Sylvia Main, his partner for the dance, standing with her sister on the gravel drive by the steps leading up to the Big House.

'You were supposed to be here twenty minutes ago, Robert,' she said, admonishing him gently, 'the drinks reception has already started.'

'I'm sorry, but it's a lang story, I'll tell ye when we get in,' said Robbie, taking Sylvia by the hand and pecking her on the cheek.

'Robert, what on earth is that on your hands; are those fish scales?' said Sylvia recoiling from his touch.

'Err, it's a wee bitty complicated...but I think we'd best get in,' said Robbie looking nervously over at Corbie who was round by the side entrance of the house talking to Alan Thain who was both caterer and master of ceremonies for the evening.

As Robbie hastily ushered Sylvia and her sister into the

main hall of the house, Alan Thain lowered the tarpaulin back onto the bed of the pickup.

'How many have you got?' he asked.

'Twinty or so,' said Corbie. Alan Thain turned to his head chef.

'Will the steaks keep?'

'Aye, nae problem, I'll jist pit em back in the freezer,' said the chef, taking a puff of his cigarette.

'And can ye get them ready in time?' The chef thought briefly then nodded.

'We've got mair than an oor til the mains gan oot; it'll be fine.'

Alan Thain smiled and pulled out the large roll of twenty pound notes he kept in his hip pocket.

'Right then, Corbie, how much do ye want?'

*

'Have you washed your hands?' whispered Sylvia as the barman poured Robbie's whisky. Robbie held his hands out to show Sylvia, who smiled and slipped her hand into his as Alan Thain appeared on the small bandstand at the far end of the hall and tapped the microphone. Satisfied that it was working, he addressed the crowd.

'My Lords, Ladies and gentlemen, I'd like to welcome you all tonight to the Summer Garden Party. As I'm sure you're aware the event is in aid of the local hospice, an excellent cause of which the Laird and his Lady wife are both trustees. So, to that end there will be several fundraising events throughout the night, including a raffle, featuring a first prize of a year's supply of Baxter's pickled beetroot, and a second prize of two year's supply of Baxter's pickled beetroot. No, no that's only a joke, we're very grateful for their support,' said Alan Thain, waving apologetically at the top table, 'oh yes, and before I go there's just one small adjustment to the menus on the table, just to say that the beef is off and we'll be having some salmon with our beetroot instead. Anyway, without further ado, and, on behalf of the Laird, I'd like to thank you all for coming. I hope you have a very enjoyable evening, and that we raise a great deal of money for what I think you'll all agree is a very worthy cause.'

As they ate their meal, Corbie leaned over to Jake and Robbie and pointed at the Laird.

'He's fair enjoying that salmon,' said Corbie, chuckling, 'he'd probably choke if he kaent faur Thainny got that fush fae.'

'Taak o the divil,' said Jake, nodding in the direction of Alan Thain who swept up to the top table carrying a bottle of wine.

'Alan, good, I'm glad they could get you…you wouldn't mind settling a dispute I have with my wife, would you?' asked the Laird.

'No, that would be no bother at all, no bother at all,' said Alan Thain unctuously, 'what would be the nature of your, erm, dispute?'

'Well, I'm of the opinion that was wild salmon we just ate, but my wife believes it was farmed. She doesn't think I can tell the difference,' said the Laird, looking down at the remains of his main course.

'Unfortunately, sir,' said Alan Thain, casting a nervous glance at the Laird's wife, 'it is farmed salmon.'

'Oh, I see,' said the Laird, looking a little embarrassed.

'Well, at least that's cleared that up,' he said, pushing the plate away from him.

'Some white?' asked Alan Thain, showing the Laird the label of the bottle he was carrying.

'Mmm, yes I will, thank you,' said the Laird.

'And for your wife?'

'No thanks,' she said, putting her hand over her glass.

'Oh, you should, it's a very good vintage, I chose it myself,' persisted Alan Thain.

'Well I would, but I'm pregnant, so I can't,' said the Laird's wife smiling at Alan Thain.

'Oh, really?'

'It's very early days,' said the Laird tersely, glaring at his wife, 'and I'd prefer it if you didn't spread it around…' he added, realising the futility of his words as he spoke them.

*

After the meal, the tables were moved to the side of the room to make way for the dancing, and as Sandy danced a St Bernard's Waltz with his wife Meg, the rest of the Summer Crew stood at the bar.

'Weel boys,' said Robbie, raising his glass, 'I'd like te thank ye aince mair fur backing me up wi the poachers, particularly you Neil; that wis brave.'

'It was nithing,' said the Neap looking a little embarrassed, as the rest of the Summer Crew toasted him.

'Aye, yer real salmon fishers noo, boys,' said Robbie, 'wi calluses on yer hands and muscles in yer erms. Look at ye Neil, you must o lost twa stane in the last three month, they'll nae be crying ye the Neap mich longer if you keep the kyte doon.'

The Neap nodded. 'Aye, but the werst o it is that I've got te buy a hale new set o claithes, ma aull een's are oer big. It's costing me a fortune.'

As the salmon fishers laughed Corbie appeared looking slightly furtive.

'I've got the money fae Thainy,' he said reaching into his pocket.

'Robbie, here ye go, here's £40 fur you seeing as ye hid to taak on the Stot.'

'No, I couldna; pit it in the collection fur the hospice.'

'Really?'

'Aye, pit it in the collection, it widna sit richt wi me. But dinna let that affect you boys.'

'I winna,' said Corbie slipping his share into the breast pocket of his suit. Robbie shook his head; Corbie turned to the three younger members of the Summer Crew.

'Neap, ye winna say no will ye?' said Corbie.

'Aye, Corbie, I will in fact,' replied the Neap sounding annoyed, 'I'm needin something ither than the money.'

'Fit's that?' asked Corbie.

'Like Robbie wis saying, I'm needing ye aa te stop crying me Neap or Neapy or onything like that,' he said looking at the rest of the Summer Crew, 'it's nae verra nice, kaen, living wi thon name.'

Robbie nodded. 'That's fine Neil, dinna worry, I'll maak sure aabidy gets the message.'

'Fit should we cry ye then?' asked Corbie.

'Jist cry me Neil, seeing as it's ma name.'

While Corbie and the students split the money, the Laird, the Super and the Factor talked at the head table.

'So, how's the season been this year?' asked the Laird.

'Poor,' said the Super shaking his head.

'The worst yet,' added the Factor.

'You know that salmon we had tonight was farmed,' said the Laird pensively, staring into his whisky.

'Really? I would have sworn that was wild,' said the Super.

'Exactly…but I checked with Alan…with fish of that quality coming out of the fish farms, what chance do we have? How can we compete with that?' said the Laird before swallowing his dram in one gulp.

'I was in the new supermarket in Elgin yesterday, and the price o salmon was less than the white fish. Can ye imagine that 20 years ago, before the fish farms?' said the Factor as the band finished playing and Alan Thain bounded on stage.

*

'OK, before the band starts up again,' said Alan Thain after the raffle was done, 'the Laird would like to say a couple of words.' The Laird, who had made his way across the hall, took the microphone from the compere and stepped onto the small stage.

'Well, thank you Alan, I'd like to thank you and everyone for coming tonight, which I think you'll all agree has been a great success,' he said pausing, 'and, on a personal note, it's a very special night for my wife and I, because I'm delighted to say that we're expecting a new addition to the family. It's very early days yet, but I thought we should let you know. Of course we're both delighted…and I can only hope that my future heir derives as much satisfaction serving the community as I have.'

The Stingman looked at Gonzo, who frowned and shook

his head, but before he could say anything Robbie got to his feet, cleared his throat and looked down at Sylvia.

'Aye, well,' he said, addressing the Summer Crew and their partners, 'I know it's nae as big news as fit Laird hid, but I've jist asked fur Sylvia's hand in marriage, and I'm delighted te say she's said yes. I thocht you boys should be the first to know.'

The Fishers of Men

SANDY GEDDES, skipper of the Summer Crew, shuddered as he lowered himself stiffly onto the cold vinyl car seat. As he sat with the engine on, waiting for the heater to warm the car, he noticed, through the slowly demisting windscreen, the swallows gathering on the telephone wires across the road. There was no doubt about it; summer was coming to an end. In three days time, the summer netting season would be over and he'd be back to skippering the permanent crew. Then a month later, they'd be up on the electrofishing for a couple weeks before the layoff: four months of fencing, ditching, planting trees and other estate work. He couldn't complain, it was better than working in a factory like Corbie, but still, it wasn't the same as the fishing.

Fifteen minutes later, when Sandy pulled up by the bothy, he was surprised to find the coble in the water and the

Summer Crew ready to go.

'Look lively Sandy, fit time de ye cry this?' asked Neil smiling and looking at his watch as Sandy struggled out of his car.

'Aye, Neil, it's guid te see yer keen,' said Sandy pulling his pipe from his pocket as he walked towards the bothy.

'Och Sandy, ye've nae time for a smoke if we're g'te beat the permanent crew. They hid a bad day yisterday, we're less than a box ahin em noo. We've got twa days left te catch em.'

'OK, OK,' said Sandy, putting his pipe back in his pocket, 'I dinna wint fowk saying that we lost the bet wi the permanent crew because I didna let youth hae its heid.'

That morning the Summer Crew worked as hard as they ever had, shooting all the way down to the mouth and hauling back up again twice over, and though the younger boys were keen to carry on, Sandy insisted they take an hour off for their lunch to let the fish settle.

'What are you going to do when the season finishes?' asked Gonzo, as the three younger members of the Summer Crew wandered up onto the viaduct to stretch their legs.

'I dinna kaen, Corbie said he wid likely get me a job in the shortbread factory,' replied Neil as the Stingman slipped through the iron struts of the viaduct and onto the outer side of the bridge. 'Hey, fit are ye deein oot there?'

*

'To whom it may concern,' said Sandy quietly as he read the writing on the envelope the Stingman had handed him. 'Faur exactly did ye find it?' he asked, looking up at the

Stingman.

'Tucked in the struts in the viaduct, just above the Bridge Pool.'

'Go on Sandy, open it,' urged Neil.

'No, I'm nae sure it's fur us,' said Sandy.

'I'm concerned,' said Corbie, reaching over to take the letter.

'OK,' said Sandy, giving Corbie a sharp look, 'I'll open it.'

'Fit dis it say?' asked Corbie. Sandy said nothing, but handed him the letter. Robbie, who was sitting next to him, looked on. Written in an elegant, spidery copperplate, the letter was short. Corbie read it out loud,

'To whom it may concern,

God is dead and we have killed him. What remains when disbelief is gone?

Please forgive me,
Mr Alistair Michie.'

'The minister,' said Jake quietly.

'He's got a bonnie hand,' said Robbie, who was an admirer of good handwriting and hadn't digested the actual content of the letter.

'Aye, Robbie,' said Sandy, sounding slightly annoyed, 'but hiv ye actually read fit it says?' Corbie handed the letter to Robbie who read it slowly.

'Fit dis he mean?' asked Robbie when he was finished reading the note.

'The bit about God being dead is a quote from Nietzsche,'

said the Stingman who was an admirer of the aphoristic 19th century German thinker, 'but I don't recognise the second bit about disbelief being gone.'

'So, is he saying that he disna believe ony mair?' asked Robbie.

'No…I don't think that's exactly the point,' said the Stingman.

'He's saying he's killed himself, is he? He's saying that he's louped fae the brig?' said Sandy, scratching his chin. The Stingman nodded.

'That would be my guess.'

'Aye weel, fit ivir,' said Sandy briskly, refolding the letter and slipping it back inside the envelope, 'I'd say we'd better ca the police. Robbie, hand us the two-wey will ye. I'm g'te speak te the Super.'

*

When Sandy arrived for work the next morning, he found three police cars parked by the bothy. Down on the scap a large man with a shaven head and an anchor tattooed on his forearm was struggling to get into a wetsuit. Standing next to him was Sergeant Davey Hendry, the policeman from Fochabers.

'Hoo lang will it tak, Davey?' asked Sandy.

'Who knows Sandy, it's a deep pool. Mind the last time we were here?' replied Sergeant Hendry.

'OK, we'll shoot the Lower Brig Pool the noo and see fit happens efter lunch,' said Sandy.

'So does this happen a lot?' asked Gonzo as they launched the coble.

'The river taaks a few fowk ivry year, ae wey or anither,'

said Sandy pensively.

Back at the bothy, the Summer Crew ate their lunch and watched the thin trail of bubbles produced by the diver's aqualung wandering around the surface of the Bridge Pool.

'I've ayewis winted te kaen fit wis doon there,' said Robbie.

'My mither yeest te tell me that the Brig pool hid nae bottom, that it jist kept gan doon,' pondered Neil, peeling an orange and then popping a segment into his mouth.

'That's rubbish,' said Corbie dismissively.

'Aye, I kaen that, I wis jist saying,' said Neil indignantly, as the frogman's head suddenly appeared above the surface.

'Did ye see onything?' asked Robbie a couple of minutes later as the frogman shrugged off the air tanks on his back.

'Nah mate,' said the frogman, who was a Londoner, 'there's no sign of nothing dahn there apart from some big old eels and some 'oles that just keep on going...'

'De ye think that's where he is?' asked Neil.

'Could be, but I ain't got the gear to check,' said the frogman.

'OK,' said Sergeant Hendry looking over at Sandy, 'in that case we'll just have te wait. We canna search the whole river.'

'So we're OK te fush again, then?' asked Sandy. Sergeant Hendry nodded.

'It's my guess that he's been swept oot te sea,' he said looking down to the undulating, grassy tops of the ice-houses down in Tugnet and the great shingle mouth of the river beyond.

*

That evening, the permanent crew had another poor catch

and so, despite the interruption of the police diver, the next morning the Summer Crew were still only one box behind their rivals, and so great a spur was the prospect of winning the competition for most fish caught in the season that, for a second morning in succession, Sandy arrived at the bothy to find the crew ready to go. The excitement of the younger members reached near fever pitch when, as they started to haul the second shot of the day, it became evident from the weight of the net that they had a big bag.

'Keep the leads doon and the corks up,' shouted Robbie, as the crew hauled hard to get the fish in quickly before any escaped. Unfortunately, however, as the net came up onto the scap it rapidly became apparent to everyone that it wasn't fish they had caught.

Sandy looked down at the body of the minister, bloated and rank from his four days in the river. Behind him Neil was sick in a whin bush. Covering his mouth with his free hand, Corbie leaned down and cut away a lamprey which had attached itself to the minister's neck then ground it into the scap with the heel of his wader. As he did, Neil was sick again.

Two hours later Sandy and Sergeant Hendry stood by the netbox watching as the forensic team loaded the Revd. Michie's body into the back of the van.

'Thanks for the prompt call, Sandy,' said Sergeant Hendry.

'Aye weel, at least it's cleared up,' said Sandy looking over to the bothy where the Super had just pulled up in the pickup.

'Sandy, there's something I need to speak to you about,' said the Super, winding down the window of the pickup as he stubbed his cigarette out in the overflowing ashtray.

'Aye, they're just taaking him awa the noo,' said Sandy pointing at the van.

'No, it's nae aboot that,' said the Super, taking another cigarette from his pack.

*

The van carrying the minister's body pulled away down the track, followed closely by the Super in the pickup. Sandy, looking grim-faced, walked over to the netbox where the rest of the Summer Crew were chatting with Sergeant Hendry.

'Sandy, I almost forgot,' said Sergeant Hendry, opening his hand to reveal Sandy's Zippo lighter. 'I meant to give you this yesterday; the frogman found it at the bottom of the Bridge Pool.'

'Look, it still lights,' he said, spinning the flywheel with his thumb and lighting the blackened wick. Sandy nodded and took the lighter from Sergeant Hendry.

'Cheer up, Sandy,' said Robbie, 'the police hiv foond yer lighter, the een ye lost fan we wis looking fur the Monster. That's a sign, it's guid luck.' Sandy didn't reply.

'Fit is it, Sandy?' asked Robbie, 'Fit's awrang? Is it finding the minister?' Sandy shook his head.

'Is it because we're nae g'te beat the permanent crew because o a this delay?' said Neil.

'No Neil, it's nae that,' said Sandy looking at his boots, 'it's the fushing, boys. It's oer.'

'Aye, I kaen, the Summer Crew's oer the morn,' said Robbie, 'but we'll hae anither month back on the permanent crew and then there's the electro...' but before he could continue Sandy interrupted him.

'No nae that Robbie…they're taakin the hale fushing aff aa thegither the morn. That's it. Finito.'

'Fit de ye mean?' said Robbie, looking perplexed.

'The fushing rights have been bocht by the Conservation Trust; the morn's the last day o the nets on the Spy.'

The Last Shot

IT WAS RAINING heavily when Sandy Geddes, skipper of the Summer Crew, pulled up in his car outside the bothy on the last day of the salmon netting on the Spey. Sandy sat for a moment and looked out beyond the questing runnels of rain on the windscreen, down the river to the mouth where the peat black water spilled into the slate grey North Sea.

Inside the bothy, Sandy lit the stove and put the kettle on. As he drank his morning tea, the Summer Crew appeared in dribs and drabs, running into the bothy to escape the cold wind and heavy rain, the enthusiasm of the last few days forgotten. By the time Sandy had finished his pipe, Corbie still hadn't arrived, though the rain had eased considerably.

'OK boys, I suppose we'd better shoot the river,' said Sandy leaning over and tapping his pipe out on the side of the stove door.

'Fit aboot Corbie?' asked Ronnie tentatively.

'Weel, we're nae g'te wait fur him...'

'But it's aye dinging doon oot there...' said Neil. Sandy shrugged, then got to his feet and put on his donkey jacket.

About an hour later, having shot the Bridge Pool and Lower Bridge Pool, the Summer Crew were back in the bothy, drinking tea and warming themselves by the roaring stove when Corbie appeared in the doorway.

'Yer gey late, Corbie,' said Sandy as Corbie sat down. Corbie said nothing, but poured himself a tea.

'Aye weel, this is neither catching fush nor mending nets,' said Sandy after a while.

'Exactly,' said Corbie with an angry look around the bothy, 'come the morn, nane o us will be catching fush or mending nets. I telt ye we should be in the union.' Sandy shook his head, but nobody said anything.

'It's a disgrace, we're being thrawn aff the river by the toffs and the rich rod fishers; fowk fa jist want te catch the fush fur sport, so they can dress up and play aroon fur twa wiks a year,' continued Corbie, presumably angered by the fact that the Conservation Trust was mainly funded and run by significant members of the rod fishing community, many of whom were large landowners.

'Aye, but ye kaen yersel, Corbie,' said Sandy calmly, 'that a rod-cocht fush brings in oer twinty times as mich money as een caught in the nets, and that's guid fur abdy. Fur the hale community.'

'That's verra noble, but fit aboot us?' said Corby looking up and staring at Sandy.

'Aye and they've promised money to build a museum aboot the fushing in the ice hooses at Tugnet,' said Robbie, coming to his skipper's defence.

'Fit the fuck's the point o a museum? Ye're nae telling me that ye widna prefer thon ice hooses fill o fush and nae some holey aull nets and pictures o boys fa yeest te werk on the fishing…that's the prablem wi this country, it's g'te end up being ae big theme park, faur we hae te bow and scrape te rich tourists and toffs. The hale country'll be a museum… and fit kind o life is that, serving fowk fa come to see fit we yeest te dee fan we hid proper jobs?' said Corbie, get angrier as he spoke.

'Och Corbie, simmer doon, wid ye, there's nithing we can dee,' said Sandy.

'Aye there is, there's the trade union fur starters.' Now it was Sandy's turn to get angry.

'Fit guid is a union fan there's nae fush? Can a shop steward conjure up mair salmon? And even if he could, wid he kaen faur aboots they were lying? Wid he kaen fit pools te shoot?'

Corbie was not about to back down.

'Local boys hiv been taakin fush oot o the Spy since ivir it wis here, thoosands o years ago…but it's nae jist aboot fush, it's aboot wer ain rights; oor rights nae te be telt by fowk fae Edinbra or London or Brussels or faur ivir the fuck it is, fit te dee wi oor ain fucking fush,' replied Corbie, shifting the terms of the argument.

'Aye, but that's the problem, Corbie, it's nae oor fush, it's ither fowk's fush,' replied Sandy, looking flushed, 'they pey us te catch the fush fur them, and noo they've selt the rights to the Conservation Trust fa'll look efter the salmon. And they've deen aa he can te help wi getting us new jobs and pitting in the compensation. You kaen as weel as I dee that the writing's been on the waa fur the fushing fur a whiley noo.'

'These fush should belang to the fowk fa come fae here. Fan we're independent, we'll be able to dee fit we want wi oor ain resources. This is exactly why we need independence, aa the boys up here fa's been laid aff fae their jobs in the shipyards, and mines, and the steelwerks is the same. Tossed on the midden by the English toffs fa run this country,' said Corbie sullenly, as the rain, which had suddenly become heavier again, drummed against the roof.

'But we're the eens fa cocht the fush,' said Sandy, 'we're the eens responsible fur the decline in the stocks. Ye kaen yersel the numbers is doon iviry year for the last ten year. And it's nae jist us, it wis the herrin first and noo the cod and the ither white fush is the same. We've aa been oer fushing. It's the prablem wi aa us humans. We're oer greedy. We canna jist taak fit we need.'

'Aye but that's nae oor fault, we taak a fraction o the catch, ye kaen that yersel...it's the Scandanavians and Russians pilling hunners of thoosans o tonnes o salmon fae the feeding gruns up in the Arctic circle wi mile lang monofilament nets,' said Corbie, still not backing down.

'And mebbe it's the pollution, and mebbe it's the disease fae the fermed stocks that hiv escaped in te the river, but that disna change the basic fact: there's still nae fush. And even if there wis, the price of the fermed fush is that low that there's nae wey we can compete,' said Sandy starting to get angry himself.

'The point is that there should be room for ivrybidy. If it was managed richt. If someone wis staunin up fur us. But they're nae. We dinna metter up here. Fit's mair important is that the posh bastards still hae their playgrun.'

'Corbie, enough, hud yer wheest, naebidy wints te hear it,' said Sandy sternly.

'Och, this maaks me seek, the wey they jist sprung this on us. They're getting rid o us like that mony spent hens,' said Corbie, putting his head in his hands.

'Dinna worry Colin, ye'll get another job,' said Robbie, trying his best to calm the situation.

'Aye, sweeping up broken bits of shortbread aff o the factory flare fur £3 an oor fur the rest of ma fucking days,' said Corbie looking up, 'I'll be doolally afore the year's oot.'

'But ye dee that job in the closed season ivry year.'

'Aye, but only because it's fur fowr months and I kaen I'm coming back doon here te the fushing. Ye can hack onything, if ye kaen it's only fur a wee whiley,' said Corbie more quietly.

'Look on the bright side, ye could be like the minister, lying on the slab in Elgin,' said Neil.

'He's lucky, he's better off oot o it,' said Corbie.

'Dinna say that Corbie, it's nae chancey,' said Robbie.

'I notice the Super's nae shown his fizzog; left Sandy te dee his derty werk,' said Corbie looking up at the Neap.

'Hey Corbie, that's nae fair, my faither's losing his job as weel, de ye think he's happy aboot it? Working in the Factor's office fan he yeest te be een o the boys running the nets. His wis a fisher too, mind.'

'Ma hert bleeds fur him,' said Corbie sarcastically, 'he's jist the same as Sandy and Robbie, he's got a nice cushy job. It was your fucking faither fa sold us doon the river.'

'That's nae true, Corbie, jist shut yer face will ye.'

'Aye, and fit are ye g'te dee if I dinna?'

'I'll fucking shut it fur ye,' said Neil lunging at Corbie, and it was only because Robbie and Jake intervened that there wasn't a full-scale fight in the middle of the bothy.

'Mind the stove, boys,' said Jake, pushing Corbie towards the door. Corbie turned and stormed out into the rain, with Jake following closely behind him.

'What will you do, Sandy?' asked the Stingman cautiously after a couple of minutes.

'Me, Robbie, Brian and twa ither boys on the permanent crew hiv been offered permanent work wi the estate. Kaen, working on the roads, forestry, deeing a bit o fencing, fixing up the butts. Then there's the electrofushing as weel.'

'What about you, Jake?' Jake shrugged.

'I canna really afford te live on fit I get fae the croft alane, but my cousin, he's affshore on the supply boats, kaen, and he's looking inte getting me a job on the ile.'

'It's a real shame about the fishing,' said the Stingman.

'Aye weel, things change,' said Sandy bitterly.

'I mean, if I could have been guaranteed a job here, I think I might have packed in my university course.'

'What?' said Sandy, with surprising venom, 'ye'd pack in the university fur a job on the nets?'

'Yeah,' said the Stingman sheepishly, 'I mean it's a great job, you're outside, it gets you fit and strong, and then there's the otters and the ospreys. I feel like I belong here…' Sandy stared at him angrily as he spoke.

'Aye weel, you dinna kaen fit it's like at the beginning o the season in February wi the grue on the river and a northeasterly blaawin in. I've seen grown men greeting wi the caal fan they haal the nets. Richt thrawn boys fa canna even thole it.'

'Ach, come on Sandy, dinna be sae herd on the loon, if I hid the option to stay on the nets, I wid. I'd dee onything te stay. I belang here,' said Robbie quietly.

'Aye, but you're nae my age, Robbie. Mind fit it wis like fan yer back packed in, and fan ye waak up on a caal, damp morning and ye canna herdly move yer knees for the rheumatics. I'm fifty fowr and ma body's hashed fae the fushing,' said Sandy angrily, before getting stiffly to his feet and following Corbie out of the bothy. Two minutes later Sandy returned.

'Look, boys I'm awfa sorry aboot that ootburst, it's nae like me...' he said shaking his head, 'it's jist that the hale thing his got me in a spin, kaen.'

'I didn't mean to...' said the Stingman apologetically.

'No, it's nae yer fault,' said Sandy interrupting him, 'it's me fa wis in the wrang. I hope ye accept ma apology.' About ten minutes later Corbie appeared in the doorway of the bothy. He too was apologetic.

'Sandy, I'm sorry fur fit I said, I kaen you hid nithing te dee wi ony o this.'

'That's fine Colin, and mind, mebbe this'll work oot fur the best, mebbe ye'll get a job on the ile as weel.' Corbie nodded his head, 'mebbe, but's the ile's aa aboot fa ye kaen, nae fit ye kaen.'

'Aye weel,' said Jake quickly, 'noo ye've aa got that oot o yer system, mebbe I could maak a wee suggestion.'

'Fit's that?' asked Sandy.

'In my experience, at times like these the best thing te dee is te werk oot hoo te maak the best oot o a bad lot...'

*

The last day of the nets saw one of the strongest runs of that season with the fish presumably encouraged by the rain. The irony was not lost on the Summer Crew, however, they only shot the river five times in the short gaps between the heavy showers. The atmosphere in the bothy was predictably subdued, but there was no repeat of the earlier arguments, and the competition with the permanent crew, which had motivated them for the past few months was long forgotten. After the final shot, the Summer Crew boxed the five grilse they caught, stowed the nets and the oars, then locked the coble and the bothy.

'That's it boys. The end o the nets on the Spy,' said Sandy, looking down to the mouth of the river.

'It's the end o an era,' said Robbie, his spiky black hair flattened against his head by the steady rain.

'Aye, it's a sair fecht fur a hauf a loaf,' said Jake ruefully.

'Let's jist hope it's nae the end o the salmon,' said Sandy.

'Mebbe if the stocks bounce back, mebbe they'll pit the nets back on...' said Robbie hopefully. Sandy shook his head.

'No, I dinna see that. Fit ivir happens wi the fush, that's the end o the salmon nets on the Spy. No, that's it, that wis the last shot.'

*

Officially speaking, Sandy was right; the salmon netting rights were transferred to the Conservation Trust at midnight that night, however, what the official histories don't record is that at eleven o'clock that same evening three cars towing trailers pulled up by the bothy, and twelve men, working two cobles, one on each of the Upper and Lower Bridge Pools, fished through the night. Quiet and efficient, they fished the river in the same way men had done for hundreds of years before, and when the pinkish hues of dawn lightened the eastern sky they locked the boats back up, stowed the nets, loaded the boxes of fish onto the trailers and drove up the track which led from the bothy to the main road. The water bailiffs, who might easily have happened by or seen them through the night scope from their base in Tugnet, had spent the night unsuccessfully chasing two young and particularly brazen poachers who led them a merry dance up near Fochabers.

When the first dog walkers made it over the old viaduct a little later that day, the only clue that anyone had been there before them was a few silvery smears of salmon scales glittering on the scap in the soft morning light.

APPENDICES

Salmon and Salmon Netting

THE LIFE CYCLE of the Atlantic Salmon (*Salmo salar*), Scotland's only native salmon species, is one of the great natural wonders of the Northern Hemisphere.

The young salmon is born from eggs laid on the gravel bed in the headwaters of a river – usually a small burn high up in the hills. The eggs are laid in the summer and incubate for around 50 days. The small fish that emerges from the egg is called an alevin. At this point it still has a yolk sac attached which is its only source of food. When the alevin has finished with the yolk sac, which usually takes a few weeks, it starts feeding on small invertebrates that live in the burn. The young salmon, having shed its yolk sac, is now called a fry, and is typically about an inch long. The fry will remain in the burn where it was born for anywhere between one to three years until, by a mechanism that is still obscure to science, it decides that it is time for it to leave its home and explore the wider world. To do this it enters a rapid growth spurt which sees it grow to around two or three inches. The parr, as they are now known, then migrate down to the mouth of the river where they start to undergo the huge changes required for them to go to sea, because the Atlantic salmon is one of the very few fish that is anadromous, that is to say it can live in both freshwater and seawater. This is a more significant change than it perhaps seems at first sight, requiring the fish to completely alter its body chemistry to survive the much more saline sea water. This process is known as smoltification, and after it the small salmon, now called smolts, are ready to go to sea.

The salmon smolts congregate at the mouth of their home rivers in large shoals before embarking on their astonishing journey, leaving the estuary of the river and travelling over a thousand miles to the seas off the coast of Greenland where they stay for anywhere up to six years feeding on krill – a small shrimp – and putting on weight.

The Atlantic salmon is the largest of the salmon genus, and can grow very large on the rich diet in the Arctic feeding grounds. The biggest Atlantic salmon ever recorded weighed 109 lbs, and was landed in a net by the commercial salmon fishery on the River Hope on the north coast of Scotland in 1960.

Not all salmon migrate to Greenland; some stop off near Iceland, spending only a year at sea before returning to their natal river. These 'Iceland' fish are called grilse, and they mainly return in the middle of the summer – around June, July and August. The grilse 'run', as it is called, is the main reason that salmon fisheries employed extra summer crews. The more mature fish return more evenly from early spring all the way through to the autumn.

The Atlantic salmon's trip of over two thousand miles is an incredible feat of stamina and endurance, however, what makes the trip even more fantastic is that all of the fish return to the river in which they were born. If you catch a wild salmon in the Spey you can be sure it was born there and somehow found its way back from over a thousand miles away: the same applies to the Dee, the Tay, the Tweed, and every other salmon river in the country. Quite how salmon find their way back to their home rivers is another aspect of their lives that is not fully understood, though the fish have an internal 'compass' that can detect the magnetic fields of the earth which probably combines with their sophisticated olfactory system to help them 'smell' or 'taste' the chemistry of their home river.

Once it has found its way back to its home river the returning salmon has to readjust its body chemistry again before it enters freshwater and swims back upstream to the same burn in which it was born, where it will spawn and die. This final stage of the journey can take anywhere from a few weeks to a few months depending on the state of the river and the health of the fish. This part of the journey is particularly arduous as the fish has not only to swim against the stream and navigate a range of obstacles from waterfalls to weirs, but also has to do this without eating. The fact that salmon stop eating when they return to their home river has long perplexed rod fisherman who use flies and lures to simulate food, or even sometimes real food like prawns or worms. Again, scientists aren't quite sure why salmon take these lures and bait, but one theory has it that the salmon snap at them out of annoyance rather than any desire to eat.

The salmon mate when they make it back to the head-waters of the river. The female, or hen salmon, as they are known, lay their eggs on the gravel bed of the burn. These gravel beds are known as redds, and the male, or cock salmon fertilises the eggs on the redds by spraying them with sperm which is called milt.

For most salmon mating is the final act, with many of them dying in the burns that they were born in. Some, however, survive and head back down the river to the sea. These kelts, as they are now called, have turned from silver to red in colour and are much thinner than when they entered the river, however, as soon as they make it out to sea the kelts start eating and return to the feeding grounds, where they put on weight again. Some fish make this journey from the burns in the hills to the waters of the Arctic circle several times, growing to a great size as they do.

*

People have been catching Atlantic salmon in Scottish waters ever since both recolonised the country after the last ice age. In fact, it's been such an important resource for many communities that it features prominently on, amongst other things, the Pictish symbol stones of North-East Scotland, and on the coats of arms of various Scottish clans as well as those of towns and cities including Glasgow and Peebles.

Before medieval times most salmon were mainly caught using traps called yairs or cruives. Salmon netting with a coble – the flat-bottomed rowing boat used by the Summer Crew – appears in histories from around the 12th century onward, with little changing in the technology or approach in the intervening years.

There are currently four legal ways to catch salmon for commercial purposes in Scotland, outlined in a range of legislation, most notably The Salmon and Freshwater Fisheries (Protection) (Scotland) Act 1951 and The Salmon (Definition of Methods of Net Fishing and Construction of Nets) (Scotland) Regulations 1992.

> **Net and Coble** – a seine or dragnet laid by a flat-bottomed boat called a coble at either land or sea.

> **Fixed Engine** – static nets which are placed on the coast around estuaries and held in place with wooden stakes and poles driven into the sea bed. Fixed engines are checked at either low tide or hauled in by a boat if they're placed beyond the tidal zone. There were fixed engine nets round the mouths of many of Scotland's rivers.

> **Haaf and poke nets** – large handheld nets, a bit like a massive rectangular versions of a sports fisherman's keep net, which are carried out by individual fishermen into shallow waters where they stand in the current with the net waiting for the fish to swim into it. These are almost exclusively used in the shallow waters of the Solway Firth and rivers like the Nith and Annan that feed into it.

> **Cruives** – fish traps made from wooden stakes and wicker-work sometimes with a stone base. These

are now extremely rare and require special permission to operate; grants for new cruives haven't been issued for over five centuries.

In *The Summer Crew* the crews fish with a net and coble. Cobles are flat-bottomed, clinker-built boats, ie. the planks or strakes of the boat are overlapped rather than abutted one to the other. This clinker-built style of boat building is common down the east coast of Scotland and the north east coast of England. The coble's flat bottom was ideal for use on the Spey which often required crews to jump out and haul a boat over the shallow shingle 'braes' between pools, this was particularly important in the summer when the water could get very low. Cobles are also very maneuverable, and while this can make them hard to handle for the inexperienced, in the hands of an experienced crew they are extremely versatile craft, capable of fishing both on and offshore.

Each salmon crew was organised into two 'boats'. Each boat had three men in it; a man laying the net, and two oarsmen. The man laying the net, who would be the skipper in the first boat, and a senior member of the crew in the second, directed the men on the oars and paid out the net that was carefully piled up on the back of the coble. Meanwhile, the three men from the other boat stood on the shore holding the free end of the net. The seventh member of the crew, the stingman, was not assigned to a boat, and was in the coble for every shot as he was responsible for safely grounding and securing the boat when it landed back on the bank.

A 'shot', which is what fishermen call the cast of the net,

started with the coble at the top of the pool. The aim of a shot was to cast the net around as large a part of the pool as possible. Each shot started by rowing the boat quickly across the top of the pool with the aim of getting the boat as close to the bank as possible without getting caught in any rocks or overhanging vegetation. When the coble reached the other side of the pool, the boat headed downstream keeping as close as possible to the opposite bank. The men holding the net on the bank walked slowly downstream to keep up with the boat as it headed downstream. When the boat reached the lower part of the pool, it turned back upstream slightly and made for the bank it had set off from in order to close the net and trap the fish. This was the hardest part of the shot as the aim was to encircle the fish as quickly as possible and stop any escaping from the bottom end of the pool, however, the current often picked up speed as it left the pool and spilled down over the next brae, so the oarsmen had to pull as hard as they could to close the net as quickly as possible. When the boat reached the bank, the oarsmen grounded it on the scap. The stingman was first to jump out holding the painter – the rope attached to the prow of the boat. The stingman would then hold the boat as the netsman and oarsmen, holding their end of the net, jumped out. The stingman then beached the boat on the scap, and joined the rest of the crew hauling in the net. The two boats, holding either end of the net would them come together until standing almost side-by-side, hauling in the net carefully to ensure that the leads were kept down and the corks kept up to stop the fish either escaping under or over the net.

When the fish were landed they were dispatched by a

short stick that each of the fishers carried called a 'priest'. The fish would then be placed in the gunwales of the boat and the boat hauled up the bank back to the head of the pool. Hauling was a relatively simple process: a long tow rope (roughly 70 ft) was attached to the prow of the boat and all of the crew except the stingman got in line, faced upstream, put the tow rope over their shoulders, and started walking upstream hauling the coble behind them. While the crew hauled the coble, it was the job of the stingman to keep the boat off the edge of the bank and ensure it wasn't damaged by rocks or caught in tree roots. This was done with the sting, a 15-20ft Scots pine trunk stripped of bark and sharpened to roughly the diameter of a broom handle at the sharp end. The stingman pushed the sting into a space under the rowlock and leaned on the other end to push the boat out from the bank.

When the crew arrived back at the bothy, the fish were unloaded and 'boxed' in fish boxes that were kept under lock and key in the netbox.

Each shot took about 20 minutes from beginning to end. And there was usually a break of about 40 minutes between each shot to allow the fish scared down the river by the previous shot to move back upriver into the pool. While the crew waited between shots they would mend any holed nets, maintain the coble or help keep things running smoothly by cutting wood for the stove or tidying the bothy. However, there was rarely enough work to fill the breaks between shots, so they were, within reason, free to do what they wanted to do.

On the Spey the crews mainly fished the Bridge and Lower Bridge Pools which were big and easy to fish and had been cleared of unwanted vegetation to make hauling easier. Around once a week the crew would put the coble on the tractor, drive up to near Fochabers and then fish all the pools down. The crew liked this as there was no hauling to be done, and it provided a bit of variety. Occasionally they also fished down from the bridge to the mouth, which they tended not to enjoy quite as much as they rarely caught much down there and sometimes had to haul the boat all the way back up.

At the end of each day, the fish were taken down to Tugnet where they were stored in the grass-roofed ice houses until the wholesalers and dealers came to transport them down south to Billingsgate and the other big fish markets of the south.

*

At its peak in the 19th and 20th centuries salmon netting directly employed thousands of people across Scotland, and sustained many small coastal communities. However, a large part of the inshore salmon fishery in Scotland was bought-out or closed in the space of about ten years around the turn of the Millennium, with the culture, tradition and skills of the salmon fishers disappearing almost overnight. There are still some working salmon fisheries, but those that do survive are under pressure and may not be around for much longer. This rapid disappearance of the Scottish inshore salmon netting industry was a direct result of the significant decline in the numbers of Atlantic salmon returning to Scotland's rivers, and consequent declines in catches.

Since the late 1980s, which is when *The Summer Crew* is

set, the Atlantic salmon population has declined dramatically. Scientists estimate that around 1,250,000 Atlantic salmon returned to Scottish rivers each year in the 1970s. In the late 1970s and 1980s there was a sudden decline in returning fish numbers with only an estimated 750,000 fish returning by the late 1980s. There was a small recovery in stocks after the turn of the century, but the overall trend has been downward ever since. In the past ten years that decline has accelerated and it is now estimated that as few as 350,000 fish return to Scottish rivers each year: just over 25% of the total that returned 40 years ago. Estimates of the global population of Atlantic salmon for the same approximate period suggest that the overall population dropped from 10 million to about 3.4 million. It's worth noting, however, that though the Atlantic salmon population from the 1970s is now considered the benchmark, the Atlantic salmon population then was almost certainly much smaller than in previous generations. This is an example of what marine biologist and fisheries expert Daniel Pauly calls 'shifting baseline syndrome', which is our gradual acceptance of new norms for population size as we forget the abundance that came before.

The dramatic decline in the Atlantic salmon stock is attributed by scientists to two main causes: offshore fishing in the feeding grounds and climate change.

It is probable that offshore fishing had the earliest impact; at some point in the late 1960s commercial fisheries discovered the location of the salmon feeding grounds in the seas of the north and soon after factory ships with mile-long monofilament nets were catching more in a day than an onshore salmon netting crew could catch in a season. In the late 1990s these offshore fisheries off Greenland and the Faroe Islands were all but closed down, however, they had a great impact in the twenty or thirty years in which they were operational.

In more recent years, climate change is thought to have an increasing influence, with warming waters in the Arctic affecting the numbers and distribution of krill, the small shrimp that is one of the salmon's most important food sources.

*

Salmon netting has, since at least the rise of sports fishing with rod and line in the Victorian era, been a contentious subject. Augustus Grimble (no, I didn't make him up) says of the nets on the Spey in *The Salmon Rivers of Scotland (1902),*

'Into the netting question I do not intend to enter.'

Before proceeding in the very next sentence to jump in feet first.

'Spey, like all the rivers, has been gradually going back, both in the yield to nets and rods, although as a matter of fact it has not gone down so much as many rivers in which there are no nets. In my humble opinion it is not any given; nets that are reducing the salmon fisheries to extinction, but it is the vast and ever increasing number of fixed engines working round the whole of the Scotch coasts that are the cause of the mischief.'

This is, of course, just Grimble's opinion and he is perhaps not the most impartial of witnesses as he was the guest of the Duke of Gordon who leased the netting at Fochabers to which Grimble refers. However, the specifics are less interesting than the fact that even a hundred years ago the decline in salmon stocks and the role of netting were a matter for debate.

I am not a fisheries scientist, however, there is little doubt that onshore salmon fishing has had an impact on stocks over the years, however, it has been estimated that onshore salmon netting only ever took a maximum of about 15% of the salmon that reached the river in any one year (which is, in turn, only a small percentage of the overall stock at sea). The onshore fisheries were a much more sustainable fishery than the offshore fisheries that sprung up and had such a significant impact in such a short time, but onshore salmon fisheries are much more visible than the offshore boats or climate change, and so have, in my opinion at least, had to carry an undue share of the blame for falling stocks.

Despite the relatively small impact of the inshore salmon fisheries there is little prospect of salmon netting being reinstated in the places in which it used to operate as long as stocks of Atlantic salmon remain so low, particularly as each rod-caught fish adds thousands of pounds to the local economy when a net-caught fish adds a fraction of that value.

It may, in the future, be possible to develop a sustainable Atlantic salmon population that allows offshore, onshore and sports fisheries to each take a fair share while maintaining overall stocks, however, that would require the type of concerted international agreement and action that seems in short supply in recent years, so it seems much more likely that we will, instead, have to implement further conservation measures as so many stocks of our marine wildlife are so seriously depleted by overfishing.

*

It's all too easy to dismiss the decline of the Atlantic salmon population and the impact this has had on small fishing communities across Scotland as a relatively minor, local issue; something that doesn't matter a huge amount in the grand scheme of things. Unsurprisingly perhaps, I don't see it that way. I think the demise of the onshore salmon fisheries asks much bigger questions about how we manage our natural resources, protect our communities and preserve our national heritage and identity. It is, of course, vital that we conserve our wildlife, but how do we also protect our communitities and their traditions?

And this isn't just an issue facing our fishing communities: climate change and the efforts to protect against it are going to have widespread impacts for many people who live and work in our countryside. For example, what happens to hill farmers if, as seems likely, Government brings in new land use laws and regulations to offset carbon? What impact will these laws have on the big sporting estates? And what about rewilding? An attractive concept to city dwellers, but what does it mean for people who live and work in the country?

These are complex issues and I can't pretend to have the answers, but what I do know is that the dramatic decline of the Atlantic salmon is a perfect example of the types of environmental challenge that will only proliferate and escalate in the 21st century if we continue to ignore our multiple impacts on the environment. Challenges that are, unfortunately, going to have the greatest impact on those people without access to wealth or political power; people like the salmon fishing communities that lived and worked round our coasts.

Glossary

THE LANGUAGE SPOKEN in the North-East of Scotland, from roughly Aberdeenshire to Morayshire, is known as Doric, which is one of the three extant native languages of Scotland, along with Scots and Gaelic. Doric is closely related to Scots, and has loan words from Gaelic, but remains a separate language which is still widely used in many communities in the North-East of Scotland.

The name, Doric, is from classical Greek – the Oxford Companion to English Literature explains the link:

> 'Since the Dorians were regarded as uncivilised by the Athenians, "Doric" came to mean "rustic" in English, and was applied particularly to the language of North-East Scotland.'

The pejorative nature of the name reflects what is a wider

antipathy towards Doric. Like both Scots and Gaelic, Doric was persecuted for much of the 19th and 20th centuries. Children were often humiliated, punished or even beaten for using Doric in school, and when they left they had to make sure they modulated or refrained from using it in certain situations, particularly when dealing with authority figures. This persecution is reflected in the way that the characters in *The Summer Crew* use Doric – some of the older men switch to English, 'gnepping' as it's called in Morayshire Doric, when interacting with authority figures like the Laird or Minister, and the students use it much less than some of the other members of the crew as speaking Doric wouldn't be acceptable in a University setting.

Fortunately, Doric is now being promoted rather than persecuted in schools, and it remains well used in many of the communities of North-East Scotland despite centuries of suppression. However, Doric speaking faces new pressures from the influence of mass media and the economic forces that see many Doric speakers leave the area. Our indigenous languages are an important part of our national identity. Hopefully books like *The Summer Crew* can help, if only in a small way, ensure that Doric remains a living language.

*

There are several distinct sub-dialects within Doric, with the characters in *The Summer Crew* speaking Morayshire Doric rather than the more widely known Buchan or Aberdeenshire dialects. I've tried to stick with what passes for standardised usage, however, Morayshire Doric has some notable features which aren't well represented in the more common Buchan- and Aberdeen-based orthographies. Therefore, in an attempt to represent the Morayshire dialect more accurately, I've gone for phonetic spellings where I've felt it necessary.

If you want to know more Doric and Scots, the fantastic Dictionary of the Scots Language (https://dsl.ac.uk/) is a good place to start. Otherwise, here's a short glossary to be going on with.

aa – all
ahin – behind
ain – own
ane – one
aull – old (Morayshire Doric)
auld – old (Scots)
auller – older
awfa – awful, but commonly used to mean very
baith – both
bide – to live, to reside, e.g. I bide in Moray = I live in Moray
black affronted – embarrassed
bleezin – literally blazing, figuratively drunk
bogey – trailer
brae – generally a hill or, in the context of the salmon fishing, the shallow water running over the drop between pools in the river
brasher – forester who strips the branches (brash) from trees when they've been felled
breeks – trousers
breenge – to plunge or make a violent effort
broo – the dole (a contraction of bureau from Labour

Bureau)

buttery – a small pastry roll with a high fat content particular to the east and north-east coasts of Scotland. Similar in taste to a croissant. Also known as a rowie.

byre – barn

ca – chop or knock

caal – cold

ca canny – take it easy, calm down

chancey – lucky

cheil – a lad

clipe – tell tales, grass

cloot – cloth

Clochan dichter – a dock leaf

cocht – caught

corbie – crow

cowp – fall

cowpit yow – literally, a female sheep which has fallen over, often used in the figurative sense to mean someone who is extremely drunk as fallen sheep can struggle to get back to their feet.

crack – what's going on, what's exciting or newsworthy

cry – call

Cymag – (not Doric) a poison used by unscrupulous poachers to kill salmon

dee – do

deen – done

dein – doing

dyke – wall

div – do

dook – swim

dram – a shot of whisky

dreich – miserable, bleak or bleak weather

drookit – wet

druth – thirsty or, by extension, a drunk

dubs – mud

dunt – hit, heavy blow

ee – eye

een – one

fa – who

fae – from

fan – when

fankle – tangle or mess

fash – trouble

faur – where

feart – scared

fecht – fight

feil – stupid, crazy

first fit – first foot, the tradition of visiting neighbours
    after midnight on Hogmanay

fit – what

fit like – how do you do?

fizzog – face, early 19th C. abbreviation of physiognomy

fou – very drunk (pronounced foo)

fowk – folk, people

fowr – four

ge – going, in Morayshire doric the consonants in
    gan or gin are often, but not always, swallowed to
    a hard 'g' sound (not gee)

gey – very (the ey is pronounced eye rather than ay)

glaikit – stupid

gless ee – glass eye

gnepp – to talk 'properly', i.e. in standard RP English, often to an authority figure

gow – gull

gowk – literally cuckoo, figuratively idiot

greeting – crying

grue – broken ice

grippet – parsimonious, tight

haar – sea mist

hack – endure

hairst – harvest

hale – whole

hauns – hands

havers – tall tales, lies

heider – lunatic, idiot

herdy scone – tough person

howp – drink

hud – hold

hud yer wheest – be quiet

hurl – to move quickly, to give a lift (in a car or on a bike)

ile – oil

jack – give up

jingbang – crowd, group

jotters – sacked, from when tradesmen would be given back their professional papers when let go from a job

kelt – a female salmon which has spawned

kinlin – kindling, small sticks for lighting the fire

kist – chest

kyte – stomach, belly

loon – boy, lad

loup – jump
lug – ear
maak – make
mell – beat or hit hard
midden – tip, dump, spoil heap
muckle – many or large, also meikle
neap – literally a swede (turnip), figuratively an idiot
near – almost
numptie – idiot
pair – poor
park – field
pey – pay (the ey is pronounced eye rather than ay)
piece – sandwich, though can be used more generally
  to mean lunch
pooch – pocket
priest – the short stick, sometimes weighted with
  lead, used to kill the salmon.
puckle(y) – a few
quine – girl, lass
rammy – a fight
randan – a night out, a binge (presumably from the
French randonnée meaning walk)
raxxed – stretched, broken
Redder – Red Lion, a public house in Fochabers
redd up – tidy up
roch – rough
rooked – bankrupted, cleared out
rowp – a farm clearance sale
sae – so
sair fecht fur a hauf a loaf - a hard fight for very little
  reward (literally a half loaf of bread)

sark – shirt

scap – the shingle banks of the river

seek – sick

selt – sold

sharn – excrement, dung

shilt – horse

shot – one cast of the net, hence the verb to shoot the river means to fish the river

skitters – diarrhea

skelp – hit

smirr – a fine rain, lighter than drizzle heavier than mist, probably from the Dutch 'smoor' meaning mist

snaw – snow

spate – river flood / high water

spier – ask, demand

spondulicks – money (from the ancient Greek, not Doric)

spurdie – sparrow

Spy – locals pronounce Spey as Spy rather than with the hard ay used elsewhere

stramash – uproar or fight

stot – a castrated bullock, also to hit generally, more specifically headbutt

stots and bangs – uneven progress

stotious – very drunk

swick – trick or cheat

swack – lithe, nimble

swally – drink, typically Scots rather than Doric

taak – take

teuch – tough

telt – told

Glossary

the morn – tomorrow
the morn's morn - tomorrow morning
thole – endure
thon – that
the noo – now, just now
thrawn – stubborn, obdurate, tough
toff – upper class person, short for toffee-nose
   (British slang)
Turra – Turriff, a town in Buchan
wer – our
wheen – a lot
wheen o havers – a lot of nonsense
wheesht – shush, be quiet
wid – wood, forest or by extension forestry
wider – waders
wifey – woman, married or not
yaldie – a brown trout
yees – use
yow – ewe

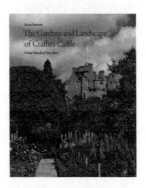